Published by: Cinnabar Moth Publishing LLC
Santa Fe, New Mexico

Cover Design by: Ira Geneve

ISBN-13: 978-1-962308-09-0

Library of Congress Control Number: 2024931815

Timeslayers

COLIN SEPHTON

For Sarah, Joshua and George,
for putting up with me… and my books!

Acknowledgement goes to Helena Blavatsky,
Robert E Howard and Michael Moorcock.
I couldn't have done it without you!

Chapter 1 – Forewarning

Isambard Hastings Raffles Ignatius sat hunched over the dusty little book. Any passer-by who cared to look would have wondered how he could see what he was reading, for he sat in the darkest recesses of the library, blending in with the shadows. He was barely within the actual reading room, but over the years the staff had become used to his eccentricities and so didn't insist he move back into the light.

It was a cold, dark afternoon, and storm clouds eddied across the sky, mixing with the smog from the automata factory on the outskirts of the city. An almost ominous atmosphere swirled and engulfed the golden spires of the city. Winters in Oxford are seldom severe, but a cold darkness had fallen upon the city. The man was oblivious to the encroaching weather. His fingers flitted across each page of velum, devouring words written in some obscure language. As he turned the pages of the ancient book he had obtained some forty minutes earlier, a faint birthmark was just visible on the back of his right hand. It was brown in colour and looked almost like a tattoo of an eye, although such a fanciful image had never actually crossed the man's mind. He had grown up with it; to him, it was just a mark, although recently this mark had started to make his hand tingle. He was sure it was the birthmark causing this. Strangely, it seemed the sensation in his hand increased depending on what he was reading in the book. It must have been his imagination.

From time to time as he continued his research, he glanced up, surveying the dons and students around him. He couldn't be too careful.

It is said that some books, some secrets, do not permit themselves to be read. For that reason, there were only a handful of people in the world who could recognise the script Ignatius was studying. He had no idea whether any members of the Administorium could translate this script, but he wasn't going to take any risks.

The Administorium were the last remnants of the ecclesiastical institution that had started Oxford University during the Middle Ages, and a small but prominent number of the current university dons were still exponents of the original system. They were a stern group with an intimidating presence. They had appointed themselves the position of keeping the balance between the old ways of the Empire and the development and influence of new and emerging technologies that might harm the Empire. Secretly, they were particularly interested in technologies that might result in a loss of power for the Administorium.

An imposing figure in traditional University robes stood blocking the only light Ignatius had, faint as it was. There were very few features to be seen within the black silhouette, only the man's mouth and tip of his nose. A whispered rasp of a voice could be heard. "I've observed you, Ignatius. You study some curious material."

Intimidation, thought Ignatius. He could tell the man was bluffing. The Administorium went in for theatrics, and that's exactly what this was. Ignatius knew he had been careful not to give any indication of the mission his Chapter were about to embark on.

"I'll bear that in mind." He had no intention of explaining himself, and the figure skulked back off into the shadows. A door clicked shut across the far side of the library, signifying the man had departed.

Glancing around cautiously, Ignatius could see that nobody else in the library had moved, gestured or even looked. He looked back at the book he was reading. He had to concentrate on the unfamiliar text to translate with any accuracy. Its author, Enoch Slipnot, had an unsteady hand, and the inks was faded in places. As he read the next section, his right hand began to tingle, a slight burning sensation.

It came through the Land of the Duranki. Those trained in the art of Al Kimiya brought forth sentient life, the fiery whirlwind that passes like lightning through the fiery clouds, believing they could master this Unholy Great One.

I have read of the great horrors the Unholy One brought forth, seeking the emerald tablet thought to have been hidden in the library of the Mystorium by the Order of the Ti-Botta. If this great red shadow should discover the sword of great power, he will wreak destruction on a cosmic scale and the whole cosmos shall tremble at his feet. The great runesword has been forged with an edge keen enough that it may even cut through the aether. Only a being in harmony with the cosmos can make use of such a weapon and with the Great Book, Turiya and the power of the Charon, summoned by the High Priest, stop the Unholy One.

I am unswerving in my task as the last remaining warrior-priest of the Charon – the Dragon- slayers of the Ecclesiarchy...

He ran his hand through a shock of blonde hair that looked

permanently wind swept. Isambard Ignatius was a tall young man; he was handsome, dressed in a frock coat of check tweed and an engineer's waistcoat, complete with a large silver pocket watch and chain.

From previous research, Ignatius had discovered a vague reference to an archaic manuscript that was said to hold the key to reality, the story of the whole cosmos – what had been, what was and that which was to come. This was said to be the biography of the cosmos. Legend had it that the book was unique in being older than the earth, indestructible, and that whoever read it could see the events described within pass before their eyes. Ignatius didn't believe this but did believe that in the wrong hands the book could be very dangerous.

Ignatius was beginning to realise that the body was, as many eastern aesthetics had taught through the ages, surplus, just a vehicle for the mind. This was a philosophy and science that would make religion obsolete. The view that the real world was nothing more than the physical world was destined to come crumbling down and be lost in the debris of all religious buildings. He knew this was why the Administorium were trying to keep an eye on his activities.

He also knew that, potentially, the Empire would amount to nothing if this book fell into the wrong hands. Circumstances in the Sudan, the Americas and the Far East had all affected this great nation and its fortunes. The Empire was perhaps at its weakest at this time. Conversely, it might even bring fortune to the Empire. Ignatius knew not.

His hand was still causing him some pain. He had never experienced this before. He sat back. He had much to contemplate, not really knowing what all this meant and not understanding how it related to the great book he still needed to find.

He closed the lesser book and carefully placed in in the repository for collection by a librarian. Having finished for the day, Ignatius checked his pocket watch and headed for the door. He stepped outside of the Radcliffe Camera with a swagger of his cane, walking through the gate and into Radcliffe Square.

Chapter 2 – En Garde!

Before him, an all-too-familiar sight: his opposition, dressed from head to foot in white, barely discernible through the gauze of his own mask and the dim light of the hall. The gas lamps flickered in the air, disturbed by the vigorous movement beneath, their dim light concealing the grandiose of the room and casting yellow light on the black and white chequered floor. The heat was rising beneath the bib of his mask, and he wanted to finish this quickly so he could catch some air.

He thrust forward, feeling the lightness of his well-balanced foil. His opponent tried to push the blade aside but failed. There was a small acknowledgement by a nod of the head and his opponent stepped back, leaving the safety tip of the blade in mid-air. A target must be hit with the tip of the foil; a touch with any other part of the blade had no effect whatsoever, and fencing must continue uninterrupted.

He made an advance, followed immediately by a lunge; his opponent met with a beat parry, striking the blade aside using the strongest part of the blade. They swiftly followed with a reprise attack, a short forward recovery and an immediate second lunge, connecting the safety tip with his torso.

The two white figures stood apart and performed the salute, a gesture of respect and civility performed with the weapon.

His opposition quickly drew off the mask and rich dark curls fell out about her shoulders. Sweat glistened on her brow, and she smiled at her instructor.

"Thank you, Monsieur Girard. I am much better, *non?*"

M. Girard removed his mask, revealing his tiny black eyes and waxed moustache. "*Mais oui, Mademoiselle!* Same time next week?"

"Of course," she replied. "But I must run, or I'll be late!"

He watched the slender figure of Indigo Gemstone hurry from the hall, removing her gauntlet and unbuttoning the croissard of her jacket as she went. She quickly changed into a tight figure-hugging shaped jacket of Harris Tweed, giving her an hourglass figure. A low round-necked knitted Fair Isle patterned dress covered her white lacy blouson, and her long legs sported Argyle patterned knee-highs and high-heeled Oxford brogues.

Although she was weary, she knew that she must hurry or miss her rendezvous in Radcliffe Square. It wasn't far from the college to the city centre, but she needed to freshen up and make herself respectable, and so headed for her rooms. She worked at St George's College, specialising in antiquities and ancient texts and was something of an enigma. Nobody even knew if her peculiar name was real.

Indigo's independence, swordsmanship and determination was the result of her childhood. Although English by birth, she had been raised partially in France. Her father and mother were of aristocratic blood, and whilst her mother remained at home raising a family, her father was an adventurer, an explorer who found home life too mundane. He was often absent but, on his return, would tell tales of the places he had been, the lands he had explored and the terrible horrors he had experienced in those far off lands. His adventures were not always appreciated by his peers at the Royal Geographical Society. It was one of these adventures from which her father never returned, and there was talk at the time of some obscure scandal. Nobody knew whether her father was still alive. Indigo had idolised her father and had grown up longing to follow in his footsteps. Maybe the scandal was why Indigo adopted the name of Gemstone. But, again, nobody really knew whether this was a pseudonym, and Ignatius had never enquired. She wondered what her father would make of all this, particularly the adventure she currently found herself in.

Before long, she had freshened, adjusted her hair and changed her clothing for more suitable attire for a lady. She left via the main entrance, her ruffle skirt swishing behind her. She gave good wishes to the porter as she went, glancing around to take in both sides of the street to check whether she was being watched. She had to be careful: the Administorium had spies everywhere, who might be following her as they had been following Ignatius.

In the centre of the city stood the Administorium, a dark monolith that looked out of place amongst the mellow Cotswold stone of the rest of the city. The mythology surrounding it claimed it was built from fire rock that had fallen from the sky; it was metallic black and etched with criss-crossing lines, which looked almost like runes all over its surface. The building was such an imposing edifice nobody dared to venture near it unless summoned – even the airships in the vicinity flew well clear of the building.

On top of the monolith stood a model of the world, carved out of rock crystal and held by what, on a bright day, looked like a gigantic set of heavenly wings. In darker weather, it seemed as if they were choking the entire world. Every so often, a vent of steam erupted from the top of the building, surrounding the winged icon in a shroud of mist.

It was here that serious menacing agents tried to shape the future of both the University and the Empire.

Many fellows in the other colleges kept their research secret, not wanting to draw attention to themselves – the agents of the Administorium, the Governors, had been known to steal promising work, either to use it themselves or keep it from the world. The Administrators were not always in favour of progress, especially if that progress was linked to studies of the mind, consciousness, the division and nature of time or the ethereal aspects of life and religious belief. They were concerned that such advancements in knowledge would lead to acceleration of the End Times, the End of Days, that the Tribulation would be brought about sooner than expected. They believed that certain studies were akin to alchemy of the highest order and would result in a disturbance to their power and their influence on the Empire.

Their compromise was steam power. It made sense to use a natural energy source. But they were concerned about recent developments to produce weaponry, and more so about the attempt to create a mechanical humanoid. Such heresy could not and would not be tolerated. The Governors believed that to try and replicate a living soul with consciousness was a gross sin against nature. The mind of a machine could never be allowed to compete with the human mind.

Worse still, the study of steam and clockwork automata was already being superseded by the students of Tesla with the study of telautomatics. It was even rumoured that the advent of electricity was leading to a new weapon, an aether oscillator called the Teleforce.

Such blasphemy was to be opposed. It could bring about a revolution within the University and potentially spread like an infestation to the rest of the Empire.

The young woman avoided the building, but the shadow it cast down the street was a long one. Every time she passed, she couldn't help but think about how different the world would have been had the Governors banned the steam gurney, something they had seriously considered, or had they banned steam weapons.

A chill ran down her spine. The misuse of power and the potential damage to the Empire by the Administorium did not bear thinking about. Although she worked in the Antiquities department, she also had a secret existence that ran parallel, and she didn't relish a normal life without adventure, without steam power, without a good thunder-blasting steam cannon at her side.

She shook off those thoughts and headed down Turl Street, past the gentlemen's outfitters and towards Brasenose College, checking her pocket watch as she went. She would just be in time for her rendezvous.

"Ignatius." Her voice carried on the cold air as he approached. "Any news?"

"Hello, Indigo." He lowered his voice. "It's alchemy, apparently." They began to walk slowly down the street.

"It seems that whatever the danger is, it was brought about by alchemy. People messing in dark arts which they don't fully understand and certainly haven't mastered. There is a reference to a dragon which I am assuming could be metaphorical…" He frowned slightly. "And from the Land of the Duranki, wherever that is."

"And the book?" she said in a low voice as they turned down Catherine Street.

He nodded. "The book we seek holds the key. Apparently, the Charon are summoned by the warrior priests to conquer the dragon. Who knows what that means?"

Indigo faltered in her steps a little. "Charon? The Charon is the ferry man to the underworld?"

"Could be. Again, perhaps it's metaphorical. He dispatches the dragon, the evil danger, to the underworld - therefore he is Charon. But the author is precise in writing '*The Charon,*' as if they were many."

"Don't pay the ferryman until he gets you to the other side" came another voice. It was a woman's voice drifting out from the darkness. Ignatius reached for the small Derringer concealed in his waistcoat and waited as a figure emerged from the shadows. Indigo had her hand on a short sword concealed in her skirt.

"Skye!" Ignatius lowered his weapon. "What the hell are you doing? I could have killed you."

She looked like a student from the University, but somewhat weird, long-legged in a short skirt, long boots, striped stockings and a low-cut top that left little to the imagination. On her left cheek, she had what looked like a tattoo of a small heart, and her eyeshadow was dark and heavy. Her dark hair in pigtails fell around her face, giving her an air of mystery.

"Oh relax, Ignatius."

"You need to stop sneaking around and be more discreet." He grabbed her slender arm and pushed her back into the shadows. Keeping a low profile, the three of them hurried onto Broad Street and headed for Summertown. Ignatius glanced around to see if they were being watched; he even looked up, checking the air. He had a feeling they were being followed, although this was probably mere apprehension. He'd spotted a shadow above them, but it might have been an Oxford gargoyle, crouching in the darkening sky, backlit by the angry clouds.

As they arrived at the house, the curtains twitched in the next-door window. He turned the key in the lock and let the women in first. He was agitated. He did not want to be seen with Skye; this mission was too important for him to be seen with the main perpetrator. If anything went wrong, he did not want to be associated with her – but he did need to check she was ready.

Inside the hall to the house, footsteps padded quickly along the multi-coloured patterned tiled floor. This was Lambeth ,the butler and valet to Ignatius. Lambeth was the only servant Ignatius kept. And a cook, of course. Lambeth was a faithful old man who had been with Ignatius for a very long time. Although he was old, Lambeth still had a full head of hair, albeit grey. He was stooped slightly, but still very agile. His appearance was deceptive; he was still very fit and very active. Not surprising really, given his past history. He was educated at Eton and Oxford and was a personal friend of Richard Frances Burton and had helped David Livingstone prepare for his expedition to Africa. Later, He had joined the army and been a Lancer in the first Anglo–Afghan war, one of the first major conflicts of the Great Game and become a Major during the Crimea and then worked on behalf of the East India Company, gathering intelligence in the orient.

He was now butler and valet to Ignatius, although he'd helped Ignatius escape a few too many close shaves.

As Lambeth appeared out of the gloom, he said, "Good day sir. Can I be of assistance?"

"No, that's quite all right thank you, Lambeth. That will be all, you can return to your quarters for the time being."

"Very good, sir," he replied and shuffled off.

The hall was dominated by a very large gilt mirror. Ignatius stowed his cane and removed his frock coat. Indigo handed him her hat, which he placed on the hat stand next to the mirror.

They headed for the study at the back of the house. These rooms were a laboratory, an Aladdin's cave of books, curios, precision engineering instruments and mechanical gadgetry. Every so often a machine would let out a little puff of steam, and there was the constant comforting click of turning gears.

Ignatius turned to Skye, who was perched on the edge of a table. "Are you set for tonight?"

Her eyes widened. "Of course. I came to let you know that it's definitely him. I've located Solomon and I've found a way in. So tonight should be easy. If you are right and he is the latest keeper of the book you seek then we should be able to find it"

"How do you know you will be able to locate it?" said Indigo.

"Persuasion if I have to." She tapped at a steam pistol pushed into her skirt and protruding out at her hip. "I can be very, very persuasive when I have to." She let out an ominous giggle.

Indigo did not see anything to giggle about, and she grabbed Skye by both arms. She didn't suffer fools lightly and was a stickler for precision and timing. She left nothing to chance and everything to planning. She was meticulous.

"Look! You can't afford to mess this up. It needs to be simple, secretive. In and out without Solomon suspecting anything. Is that clear? There shouldn't be any persuasion. This is a stealth mission. All we want is the book."

Skye brushed Indigo's arms aside and scowled. "Crystal clear! The Union has nothing to worry about."

"See that it doesn't," said Ignatius "The Union has paid you handsomely for a single job. It has a long history of protecting the

Empire and after your mission you will always be in its protection."

Ignatius and Indigo were members of the secret organisation known as the Union Jacks. A secret organisation, invisible and omnipresent, without beginning or end, with no recognised or official recorded history. They were elite individuals of engineering, science and technology who did not honor borders. Their story was long and complex, and entwined with the established colonial history. The secret Brotherhood that preceded them traced their origins back to Brutus of Troy. The modern-day Union traced its origins back to circa 1275, obtaining a Royal Charter in 1775, their remit to defend the interests of the Empire in British America, eventually expanding to defending all the interests of the British Empire. Their number, rank and file were both unknown and unknowable. Because of this there had been no public curiosity about nor antagonism toward them among the general public. No one could either deny or verify that the Union Jacks existed. Nothing could be traced: no mention of them in the history books, no utterance, no indication of their existence, no archival records; no acknowledgement of their feats. Ignatius needed to keep it that way.

The Union was peopled by extraordinary men and women, who, down the years had helped to shape the Empire. They worked to never let the sun set, never let the shadows lengthen in their role as Imperial Guardian to maintain the natural order of things, with teamwork, loyalty and rightful authority to guide humanity through its course. At least, that was their thinking. At times, this was at odds with the self-appointed Administorium, who seemed to be trying to shape the Empire to their own ideas. It was only recently that they seemed to have taken an interest in Ignatius, but for the most part that seemed to be out of the usual paranoia of anyone they didn't really know or trust, rather than any observations of

Ignatius's actions.

"Alright. You should get going – it isn't a good idea for the three of us to spend too much time together."

"Ok." Skye made for the door. "See you soon!"

Ignatius and Indigo waited in silence as Skye left, and then Ignatius sighed. "I really don't trust her," he said. "I think we ought to be close by tonight, just in case."

He had a sinking feeling in the pit of his stomach. He knew they should never have hired her; she was unpredictable, which had been the trait the Union had thought might be useful. But who knew what she might get up to?

But then, that was what they were buying. If anything went wrong, at least it would be completely believable that she had made her own choices.

Chapter 3 – Deceit

Skye headed back to her lodgings in the industrial area of Cowley. The air was thick with pollution from the manufactories, and she had to breathe deeply at times to get enough oxygen. She preferred to lie low in the underbelly of Oxford when she did not have to convene with Ignatius. She was highly intelligent and cunning, managing to deceive Ignatius into believing that she was about to carry out his mission.

She was a member of a small, little-known, underground cult thriving in Oxford and had risen amongst its ranks to become its leader three years ago. Unknown to the other members, this was more than a harmless club. She carried the oppressive burden of a dark secret that had been the long heritage of her family blood line. A secret she had only uncovered herself recently.

It was like a giant self-destruct button had been pressed. Not content with hallucinogens and group sex whilst swigging neat absinthe from the bottle, she had begun to experiment with occult rituals and the casting of runes to determine her next actions.

Due to the circumstances of her upbringing, she had tried to find solace in all sorts of depravity to fulfil her dark cravings. She never knew her mother, who had died in childbirth. She had been left to be raised alone by her father, a clergyman from St. Mary Magdalen Church. At times, she had an uncontrollable anger, much like her ancestor Henry, apparently a dominant family trait of the Angevin bloodline of the House of Anjou. But then her wretched family line was supposedly cursed and were said to be descended from Satan himself.

The Angevin blood line stemmed from Richard I, the Lionheart, born in 1157, just a few miles away in Beaumont Palace in the heart of Oxford. The only reminder was in the name of Beaumont Street; the stone from the palace had been re-used to build Christ Church and St. John's College. Richard was famed for his callous cruelty and famed among the English for being held captive during the third crusade, his ransom paid by the Knights Templar. The king produced no legitimate heirs, and acknowledged only one illegitimate son, Philip of Cognac. But Richard also had an illegitimate daughter who, like the Pharaohs of ancient Egypt where descent was through the female line, continued the Angevin bloodline through to the present day.

Legend had it that the Templars conversed with an idol called Baphomet. But despite history recording Richard as a homosexual, he coupled with the female consort of Baphomet and an illegitimate hell spawn was produced, surviving to the current day. Hell spawn were destined to live a miserable existence, doom-trodden and self-destructive. An infestation upon the earth that one day, given the right circumstances, would rise up to conquer nations. Or, at least, bring large-scale death and bloody destruction to the earth. The circumstances had not yet been quite right for a full demonic deluge, and so the blood line continued to wait and watch, ready to seize the right moment.

Since turning twenty-one, her world had been engulfed by darkness, a thick syrupy suffocating darkness that had cursed her bloodline through the centuries, with terrifying nightmares that interrupted every sleeping moment. The grubby worthless lives they were destined to lead in hopelessness. The escapism into drugs, sex and violence had not worked, offering only temporary respite. She felt ashamed, dirty and worthless but had kept enough grip on reality to work out how to end the curse that haunted her family. She had studied at the penny universities and had discovered the existence of a very ancient book that lay somewhere on the Thirty-One Planes of Existence. It was said that the pages were impervious to water, fire and air and that it was so old that its true origins were unknown. This ancient tome was the original work from which all other mystical tomes are written. It was believed that the creator, the Great Creator of the Cosmos had written it with his own hand to record creation from beginning to end. Locked within the book were the seeds of all manner of ancient manuscripts and tomes, some of which had been lost forever, and others that had come down through the mists of time. They all existed within its pages. All had been in existence since the dawn of time. Some books would endure for an eternity and some would disappear and be forgotten. Some already had vanished, and some were yet to be: such is the nature of the Creator's book.

The knowledge of how to end the hopeless self-destructive nature of her family line was within her grasp. She knew her line was destined to never die out, that it would always continue due to some devil work. Maybe that was why Richard I had turned to homosexuality. She had tried to convince herself that she was a lesbian, but after several failed affairs resolved, she knew she was probably destined to spawn some devil child, having convinced herself that she had the number of the beast imprinted on her soul.

The end of this hopeless self-destructive nature was nearly in hand. She had successfully managed to infiltrate the Union Jacks and persuaded Ignatius to trust her. She knew she had to play along with the Union's plans, secretly her mission was the same. There was no way Ignatius was going to be giving orders, thinking the mission was his for the taking. Using her as everybody else had ever done. She would find the book tonight and use it for her own means. It was time to avenge her family once and for all by using the knowledge it contained.

She first scribed the floor with runes of blackest ink, surrounding herself with the magic she believed would give her strength and energy to carry out her mission. She could find meaning in almost everything. She had always experimented with occult rituals and the casting of runes to determine her next actions. She bathed, to wash away the dust of everyday life and afterwards. Standing in front of a full-length mirror, she studied herself carefully. Upon her left breast, she had tattooed the master of all runes, the Black Sun. Her family had adopted it as their emblem. Skye was not on any mission for the Union – that was just her cover; she was looking to the fate of her own blood line.

She got dressed in improper fashion as if it were some sort of ritual befitting of her dark and devious soul. Upon her lithe form she secreted a lone gun, large calibre. The type that didn't just kill but blew large holes in its victims. And yes, tonight there would be a victim. Tonight, Skye would turn assassin to get what she wanted!

Chapter 4 – Death

The clouds were dark and oppressive above Oxford's dreaming spires. They would split every now and again to let the moonlight through, but the majority of the time an inky darkness surrounded the house. It was an unassuming melancholy grey house in Park Town, just north of the city centre, with stark walls and shuttered windows that gave away nothing of their contents. The branches of thick trees in the communal gardens creaked in the northerly wind. The night was cold, creepy, and lifeless.

A red leather-bound book lay open on the desk in front of Solomon next to a bone-handled magnifying glass. He checked his watch just as the heavy ornate bracket clock on the wall chimed midnight. Although the light was on, the study was a gloomy place. The study was a large chamber. Around the walls were hundreds upon hundreds of leather-bound books residing on bookshelves that seemed to disappear into the ceiling space. Obscure tomes, all of them. The air was dry and dusty. The only moisture evident in the atmosphere was the steam rising from his cup of coffee. A lifetime spent in books, rare and, for the most part, unobtainable. He had a room at the University, but he kept nothing like this there; here lay the secret teachings of all ages. Each book was bursting with forgotten knowledge. His life had been devoted to gaining knowledge, which could, for the most part, be considered lost to the western world. Although this was a technological age, that which had gone before, that which was once great, now even more so, had been diminished and forgotten except to a few such as Solomon.

He was the sort of man who did not rest, did not sleep, in his longing to know that which others did not, that which would never be redeemed unless by himself or a fellow like him. With the knowledge he had accumulated, he had travelled the sands of time itself. To him, a book was precious. He could hold in his hands the thoughts of an individual from a bygone age. *What sacrilege it must have been, what loss, the destruction of the Egyptian Library at Alexandria,* he thought. The text of many of his prized possessions had originated in that library. Lost to the world for centuries until rediscovered by him. For all intents and purposes, they were still lost. Although he had never been initiated into any kind of secretive order, he knew and kept secrets all the same. Some secrets, no other living person knew. He had always preferred to work and research alone. Secrecy seemed endemic in modern society, and he knew that some of the rarities he dealt in automatically led to such secrecy.

Solomon was restless. He hadn't slept properly for days, weeks. Something was wrong, but he couldn't quite put his finger on it. He felt like he was always being watched. He'd even taken to leaving the university at different times in the evening, walking different paths to get home. He was middle-aged and, due to his lack of sleep, looked dishevelled. He was a thin grey man, with receding grey hair at his temples, which only meant that more frown lines could be seen. He looked worried, perplexed. His face was haggard and lined. He wore a white formal shirt, open necked with the sleeves rolled up. His fingers were long and thin; veins protruded from his hands and ran up his slender forearms. Nothing had ever eluded him for this long.

Ignorance of the self is what had prevented humans from truly progressing; from understanding their own nature. But their works, the science of things divine and human, had been left behind for a blind race that had no notion of the power and the lost wisdom they contained. Why should it be exposed to such ignorance? Amongst Solomon's collection was an unknown book by John Dee, the eminent Elizabethan mathematician and astrologer; fragments of a priceless unknown codex by Leonardo Da Vinci; a lost Tibetan work on consciousness; a secret Gospel reputed to be in the hand of Jesus himself; a map of the Antarctic continent before the encroachment of the ice cap; an additional manuscript to the seventeen already known as the *Corpus Hermeticum*, attributed to Hermes Trismegistus; and other heretical works of great importance.

The book on his desk he was currently pondering was also a little-known esoteric work. Would this little book reveal the key to the concern that currently troubled him day and night? Even though he was fully conversant with the alchemical language of the birds, he could not make sense of what he knew to be so. This particular problem had him stumped. Solomon knew that alchemy was really the transformation of the soul, and that the subject he was investigating was connected to the soul, the very consciousness of man – the very consciousness of the cosmos. His fingers moved across the text.

Here begins the Book of thy Origin

Here begins the descent of thy soul

Here begins the descent of The Beautiful and The Damned

Here begins the Terrors

Here begins Tribulation

The codex to which this is the beginning is dedicated to a tale of wonderment and a secret doctrine concerning the inner mysteries of life and the cosmos. It bears record of the words of the Ancient Ones laid bare as testimony to the order and formulae that governs this Great Wheel of Life set in motion by the Mind of The First Cause, The Great Architect of the cosmos, The Omniscient One, whom we call The Omnisoul…

He paused. Solomon tried to work out the significance. In the eerie light of the moon that shone through the chipped window with its peeling paint, his eyes rose to meet the gaze of a stranger. A woman. She was standing in the shadows, a menacing pose, her legs astride. Poised and stable, holding a large steam pistol, pointed straight at him.

Perhaps she was part of a student prank that had come too far, thought Solomon. It couldn't be his books; no one knew of their existence. *How did she get in, though?*

"Contemplating the descent of your soul?" said Skye. "Illumination, I think, is what you need!" She laughed mockingly.

"Welcome to Aornos, the place without birds", she said, "for although conversant in the language of the birds, it has helped you none, where the Book of Consciousness is concerned. Am I correct?" she asked.

The name of that book. She was clearly conversant with Solomon's work. But how?

"I… I… don't know what you mean" Solomon said nervously. He was normally so eloquent, but he was tired, and his nerves were frail.

"Cut the pretence, Solomon" she snarled. Patience was not her virtue. Looking around at the bookshelves, she spoke, "science and magic – not too dissimilar, heh?"

She knew his name. Solomon knew he was in trouble now, despite all his precautions, all his efforts over the years. Perhaps she was just a chancer. That was the best he could hope for. He had even been successful in avoiding the attentions of the Administorium for all these years, hiding in plain sight, no one ever suspecting him of activities other than what they saw.

He hoped nobody else lurked in the darkness. Just one woman; he might stand a chance. Who was he kidding? He had not the strength or stomach for fighting right now. He was drained, physically and mentally. He nervously glanced at the weapon pointing at him. The cold steel glinted in the pale blue moonlight. Beads of sweat broke out on his furrowed brow and ran down his face blurring his vision.

"Take them! Some are worth a shilling or two." He shot a glance over at a particular bookcase to his left.

She laughed a loud, harsh mocking laugh. "Tut, tut, tut. What do you take me for, Solomon? A common criminal? A fool?"

"The rest will require specialist fencing. They are all the rarest of the rare. No one in this market will touch them" he retorted.

"Of course, I know you are right, but I'm not here to steal a few books and make a fast buck." Solomon feared the worst. *This is a contract robbery*, he thought.

She leaned forward, her oval face coming out of the shadows. She thrust the gun at him. "Now, where is it hidden?" she barked. Solomon was startled. "W…w…wha…" He didn't get time to finish.

She was cold and calculating. Solomon could feel it in the air as if she oozed cold bloodiness and death. She was not going to be trifled with. Solomon had never met a woman like her and knew she meant business

"Tell me where it is, or I'll blow you away now!" she shouted angrily. "I'll spend the next week here looking for it if I have to. You and I know no one will miss you! That's the downside of being a bookworm… worm!" She laughed coarsely at her own joke.

Deep down, Solomon knew she was right. That was the forfeit one lived with by taking the left-hand path and working in secrecy. Solomon knew that the clandestine ideas he was working upon were decidedly pagan and anti-Christian. Brought up as Roman Catholic when he was a boy, he now bore a grudge. The Church was nothing more than a web of deceit, spun to keep the masses in their place. He had abandoned the Catholic Church and had no sympathy for their sufferings; he instinctively knew there would soon be more of them. He might not be able to obtain what he wanted from the book the girl sought, but he could sense dark forces were at work. Not just the criminal minds of the country's underworld, but real, dangerous forces, the like of which no man should have to bear witness to.

He had never married, preferring instead the company of the written word and fine works of rarity and art. He had never thought of it as a lonely existence, but he had never felt quite as alone as now.

"Who are you?" Solomon asked, summoning up courage. "I don't know what you want."

A loud bang split the silent air and hot steam hissed and wafted around the room. "Next time I will," she paused "shoot you," she said. Solomon suddenly looked more haggard than before. Skye picked up the leather-bound volume he was reading, and read.

Blessed is he who readeth these words and understands the symbols and philosophy contained within of the secret processes that are recorded here as a True history of what is, will be and has always been. For he shall be of True Initiated Mind, not descended from primal earth, unseen and loathsome like the spawn of Man who came from the Dark Stars and spread across the land like a pestilence and from whose uncultured hands this Great Arcanum, this Akashic Record must, forever remain concealed locked in symbol and allegory.

In the beginning, Time was not, for it lay sleeping in the eternal embrace of darkness which filled the boundless void.

Witness the beginnings of sentient life, for here the First disclosed his real mind. At the centre of the dark matter lay a shape that may not be described and from it came bright space, son of dark space shinning forth like the divine sun, the great blazing dragon, bringer of the Threefold Fire.

The effulgency of light gave birth to reawakened energies and from the divine light emanated the forms -– the Primordial Flame and god-consciousness of the Unmanifest Absolute that worked to weave the fabric of the thirty-one planes, followed by the first seven breaths of the fiery dragon. Who, produced the fierce shining brightness that passes like lightning through the fiery clouds and thrills the universe with its whirlwind and unholy joy. Now behold Moros, swift son of the shining ones.

Behold The Charon. The great unholy ones who have come from their dwelling place to tread upon the earth and who shall put down the kings from their thrones so that they shall pretend no more and shall know their sacred self. Their symphony of music shall bring dread and death to whoever shall succumb to its harmony.

"Heavy stuff" she said. Skye looked over and checked that

Solomon hadn't moved. "I want to know where you have hidden the Book of Consciousness" she said. "Clearly, your book here is referring to it, this Akashic record, the thoughts of a higher being."

She saw Solomon's eyes involuntarily flicker and cast a quick glance to the book shelf on the right. It was the briefest of actions that he couldn't control, but enough to betray the current resting place.

"Fool" she said, striding over to the bookcase to Solomon's right. "How do I open it?" she questioned.

"I... I... don't know wh..." stuttered Solomon. She casually fired up the steam pistol and aimed at his heart. He didn't think that she would actually kill him without knowing where the book was, but was he prepared to take that chance? Solomon was in a dilemma; this had been his lifelong work. He thought for a moment. So far, he had failed. The great treasure he had owned all this while had failed to give up its secrets. Perhaps this was it. He was a failure, and his fate was to give it over to another. Before he knew it, he found himself involuntarily whispering "Ok, Ok! Book on the right, bottom shelf......" He had lost all strength in his legs. His entire body felt battered and deflated.

"Now that wasn't so bad, was it?" She drew the book out slowly. Nothing happened. She opened the book and there inside was a hollow compartment containing a large iron key. "Where's the keyhole?"

"Top shelf, behind the central book" he said. "But what do you want with it? You can't use it. It won't even open!" Solomon was now getting desperate. She was too close to the book in question.

The woman looked up. The central book was a large leather-bound volume about five inches thick and aptly titled *The Key to Destiny*. He had a sense of humour, or was it irony?

"Solomon, you have a sense of humour." She let out a gutsy

laugh, removing the book and throwing it aside. It fell open giving off a small cloud of dust. A few yellowing pages fell out and one crumbled into small fragments. "Oops, clumsy" she said with a glint in her steely eyes. There was definitely no pity in them. Solomon's face was contorted with anger.

At the back of the bookcase was a keyhole. She inserted the key and turned it anticlockwise. The sound of a huge bolt cranking split the silence. She pulled on the side of the bookcase, and it swung open to reveal a huge steel-doored vault with a combination lock.

She turned to Solomon. "Well?" she asked.

"I won't tell you," he said defiantly. He knew death stared him in the face, but he had no intention of letting her walk away with this volume. The importance of it was immense beyond all comprehension for most of the populace. But then again, Solomon had never managed to open the great tome during all the time that he possessed it, or conversely, the time it had possessed him. Its magic had kept it firmly shut, and no attempt to prise it open had ever been successful. However, for Solomon this was part of the joy of owning such a rare specimen.

Then again, with danger staring him in the face, what harm could it do? A young slip of a girl would have no chance of opening the book. That would show her, Solomon thought; and the book was so big, she had no chance of carrying it away. It had taken Solomon three days to stealthily get it into his house under the cover of darkness.

Solomon had found the book when working at the Bodleian Library while studying for his PhD. Forgotten in time, beneath St Mary Magdalen and along St Giles' Terrace there lay an ancient subterranean world of tunnels and caves that spread out beneath the city, originally an ancient gathering site with sacred significance.

Oxford always had been a mosaic of religious belief systems and philosophies. Travelling down the Woodstock Road and onto St. Giles' Terrace, just over a one-mile stretch in all, one passed a whole tapestry of religions and mixed cultural beliefs. There was a Baptist Church, a Christian Science reading room, a Quaker meeting house, St Giles' Church, the Monument to the Oxford Martyrs and the church of St Mary Magdalen.

Part of the tunnel system had been found, utilised, and expanded by the Bodleian library for storage. Solomon had worked part-time fetching books from the underground labyrinth to fulfil readers' requests. It was during this time Solomon encountered the book. The crypt in which he found it had been carved into the honey-coloured limestone. It was dark and dry with a faint mustiness to the air. The air hadn't been breathed for hundreds of years. Around the walls were curious carvings and what looked like letters of an unknown writing system. Here and there, the walls were charred with soot where torches had burned, bringing out the relief of the carvings. It was like a small self-contained shrine. The stylised carvings depicted unknown figures and scenes the like of which Solomon had never seen before. They resembled no other culture on earth, but for some reason he was sure they had religious significance.

The Bodleian Library itself had opened in 1602 with a collection of 2000 books assembled by Thomas Bodley of Merton College. It replaced the library that had been donated to the Divinity School by Humphrey, Duke of Gloucester, who was the brother of Henry V of England. In 1610, Bodley made an agreement with the Stationers' Company in London to put a copy of every book registered with them in the library. What no one ever realised was that the main purpose for this collection was not to provide a copy of every book on order to assist study, but to hide the one book that Bodley knew to be the rarest of them all. He thought that by amassing so many volumes so quickly, he would be able to secrete the Book of Consciousness until such time as he could open it and study its contents.

When Bodley left Oxford in 1576 with a licence to study abroad, he travelled Europe, touring France, Italy, and Germany, visiting scholars and adding French, Italian, and Spanish to his range of languages. It was whilst on these travels Bodley had acquired The Book of Consciousness, probably in France.

Bodley's collection of books grew so quickly the library had to have an extension to the building within two years, and another in 1634–1637. The library now contained over one million volumes and acquired over a hundred thousand new items each year, occupying several miles of shelving, much of that underground.

It was by chance that Solomon stumbled upon the oldest depths to the collection deep underground. Deep in the furthest recesses of the tunnel network, he found a dead end bricked up sometime in the seventeenth century.

Beyond the wall, Solomon found a tunnel about one hundred yards long; empty, dark and dank; forgotten to all at the library. At the end of this passageway was another wall, much more ancient. The clay bricks were crude and all slightly different sizes. More ancient than the first wall, the mortar was crumbling. It bore the seal of Thomas Bodley, along with a sign indicating that only those who are truly worthy would be able to enter beyond. Beyond the brickwork lay a crypt. At its centre stood what looked like a large sarcophagus of dry, cracked oak. The greyness of the wood indicated that it was very ancient and as hard as the rock. Within lay the book, which must be indestructible, for in the past, it had withstood a subterranean flood and the fire of 1009 when the Danes destroyed the city.

Every now and then throughout history there will be books, knowledge that is not compatible with current thinking. Texts that are thought to be heretical in some way are often destroyed. The sixteenth century saw the burning of manuscripts, witches, and heretics. So, a wise Thomas Bodley decided that, even without any knowledge of what it contained (for he never succeeded in opening it), the Book of Consciousness should be locked away safely. He knew its importance and placed it there for safe keeping in the hope that one day he would hold the key.

Very quickly, Solomon had worked out that the position of the crypt at the end of the tunnel must be near to Park Town, the street where he lived! So he began to excavate from his home, to tunnel through to the other side of this seventeenth-century wall.

It is strange the way fate works. Without any more procrastination, Solomon got up out of his chair and opened the vault, being careful not to let Skye see the combination. As the great cold solid door swung open on its perfectly engineered robust hinges, the drab study was filled with a luminous green glow.

The book lay at the centre of the vault on a low cushioned plinth. It was huge, measuring some eight feet by five feet. This was *The Book of Consciousness*, known also as *The Book of Turiya*. Its cover appeared to be made of emerald – two huge slabs of emerald with runes carved upon them. The rest of the vault was empty except for strange paintings and runes upon the walls.

Skyes eyes were wide open, as was her soft pink mouth. The book was literally bewitching. "*Hermes Trismegistus*", she said softly to herself. "The Emerald tablet. It's true. It exists." She looked around at the walls and suddenly remembered the situation she was in, snapping herself back to reality.

"Oh, very artistic Solomon", she snapped, referring to the vault décor.

Gathering strength, Solomon retorted, "They are there for a reason, fool, to protect and keep it secure! See if you can have better luck opening the infernal book than I have. Tools, weapons, even necromancy doesn't seem to work. So best of luck for all the good it will do you. Even if you could open it, the whole cosmos will conspire against you," he said bitterly.

As she approached the book, it seemed to be humming quietly. It had some kind of resonance, as if sentient. Cautiously, she touched the cover of the book. It was vibrating ever so slightly, vibrating with the energy field of the cosmos. What she could feel were the vibrations that had allowed the Book of Consciousness to manifest itself upon the same plane as the earth.

Her heart began to race so fast she thought she might pass out. She could hardly contain herself. At last, the answers to her family's curse. Her helpfulness to the Union Jacks was just a cover for her own mission. This book contained the entire history of the cosmos and would provide the answers she desired: exactly how the Angevins were cursed and how to stop the downward spiral into oblivion so that she and the rest of her future descendants could lead peaceful lives of normality, whatever that was, and die peaceful deaths.

She nervously grasped the thick edge of the book cover. Solomon looked on and sneered. Then, to her surprise and Solomon's, she magically turned the great heavy cover of the ancient tome, which fell with a great crash to the floor of the vault. A cloud of dust ascended into the air. The dark enchantment placed on her family masked her interest in the book. A book that ordinarily, according to the laws of the cosmos, she would not be able to open.

Solomon stood there, frozen to the spot, aghast and confused at what was happening. *How could she just open the book, with no effort?*

Skye felt the pages between her fingers – soft, silky, almost fleshy. They buzzed and as her fingers caressed them, they whimpered, sighed and were almost alive! She randomly but carefully turned some pages, flicking through them trying to contain her giddy excitement. A diagram, some sort of symbol, caught her eye. She stopped and flicked back to that page. It had gone. She tried again. And again. Bizarrely, the pages she had just seen were no longer there. She thought the confusion was due to her excitement, so she purposely took in a whole page. She turned it carefully, and then back again. The page was different. She did it again – a different result. Again, and again.

Her frustration was mounting, her face awash with anger. "I need to know the fate of my family, Solomon. I need to know my fate." She wanted to put an end to the suffering. Her suffering. The façade of helping the Union was just the key to achieve her objective.

Solomon's heart quickened; his breath shortened. His cold sweat had now turned to hot, excited perspiration. "The book, the book," he said "it's open! Open!" and he raced across the vault to look "All I have ever been able to do was break the seal, but never open it."

He did not consider in his rush was that he was sealing his own fate. Maybe the book had foretold it, recorded it somewhere. Solomon would never know. Shortly, the same would be true for Skye. Some philosophers and religious beliefs teach that an individual makes their own fate. Whether the Book of Consciousness actually agreed with what happened next, nobody will ever know. But Skye was to seal her own fate also, a fate that would be forthcoming sooner than she had perhaps wanted.

Whether it was out of sheer frustration, the surprise of his actions or cold malice was unclear. "Get back!" she shrieked, slamming the book shut once more as he raced over. Without hesitation, she shot Solomon in the chest at point-blank range. Blood sprayed across the study, splattering against precious books and her cleavage and face.

Solomon grasped his throat and chest. The noise he made was awful. He gasped and gargled and let out a kind of hissing sound, mimicking the hiss of the steam pistol. His eyes closed to hide his soul from his assailant, and eternal night began to envelop Solomon within its shadowy wings. Skye fell to her knees and taking a coin from between her breasts she lifted Solomon's chin. Opening his mouth, she forced the coin inside, underneath his tongue.

"He only accepts the dead if paid an obolus for their passage." She gave a cruel laugh. Then, clamping his mouth firmly shut, she let his lifeless body fall to the floor. "There, now die in peace Solomon," she whispered. The coin was meant as a cruel cold joke, a fantasy that had lived in her head for a while and seemed like a fitting idea.

What Skye didn't know was this tradition had long since passed into obscurity; and for good reason for it was the sign of a calling; a gathering of forces she would never comprehend.

This was the sign to the ferryman of the dead, Charon, in ancient Greek mythology. The coin represented payment for passage of the souls of the dead across the river Styx and into the underworld. Solomon knew the story of every mythical hero and character contained some elements of truth; most of them had existed at some time on the earth, or at least on some plane or another, and might exist again, for time and space are malleable and entangled, interwoven within the whole of creation. The cosmos is multi-layered, with unseen dimensions and in-between realms inhabited by spiritual beings and ghost worlds. It is no coincidence that many of the world's myths and religious offerings share similarities, for nearly all are based on the same mystical origins that reside on or between these other realms.

Chapter 5 – Visions of Hell

As Skye turned away from Solomon's distorted body and opened the book once more, a dark vapour began to roll into the room from nowhere. A cloudy substance containing sentient life billowed like liquid marble, liquid fire; fire from the depths of hell; a scarlet kaleidoscope. A general aura of terror filled the room, and a cold chill trickled down Skye's back. The hairs on the back of her neck bristled, and she froze in her tracks, unwilling or unable to move. She thought her heart would stop. The thick red haze continued to billow and fill even her subconscious. At times, the sentient clouds moved convulsively and seemed to create faces, twisted and tortured, which would then fade away again, only to be replaced by another, or a formless beast of some sort. The terrible power gathered, metamorphosing, and awaiting a powerful return to earth.

A mass of mosaic red gradually came into view. It was an organic mass of fire and brimstone, a sea of writhing bodies bound to each other, bound to their surroundings. An obscene formless mass of naked bodies was just discernible through the haze. A purple nebulous tide of naked sinners poured down through the darkness, yielded through time by the sickle of death. Naked flesh writhed upon naked flesh, a gruesome sea of lust: vile, bloody and dead. There were no visual signs of suffering, but the mass of sweating bodies were writhing in agony, a slight audible disconcerting moan could just be heard, with the occasional shriek.

The evil stream of gore and blood, the evil masses of bodily mud, were preying on each other's flesh. Here was a vast charnel house, full of thousands of bodies piled in an enormous heap, formed by degenerate treacherous souls confined to an eternal orgy of damnation. Here were the lustful, the gluttonous, the wrathful and the sullen, the hoarders and the wasters, the heretics and the violent.

The scene showed no bottom to the demonic pit, with licking flames rising up as if from a red burning lake. The wasteland before her was wet with rivers of blood and boiling pitch. Chaos ensued and paradise was lost. Skin was flayed and the gore quivered with heretical, blasphemous anarchy. Gender was irrelevant here. These were fruits from the forbidden tree. A considerable number of bodies merged as one shocking shameful entity.

A faint continuous dreadful weeping could be heard from the throng of flesh. Moans echoed and filled the void. The abomination held lamentation for the Ancient Ones chained within the abyss surrounded by the swarming multitude of pitiful creatures that were once human.

The crimson void became a mass of gloomy unstable colours that would occasionally break and emit rays of light, which would touch upon and mock the seething mound.

Then the rotund face of a three-eyed being appeared through the bloody haze. His eyebrows were aflame, his fiery hair leaping above him. He grinned a sinister grin with a wide-open mouth and lolloping great tongue that fell from his open lips. Although

Skye didn't know it, this was the Keeper. All he knew was that the Charon had been called, and so he was duty bound to release them from their supernatural chains in order to fulfil their fate once more.

Somewhere a sound like distant thunder roared and the colours became agitated. "He is the blazing divine dragon, bringer of the Threefold Fire," muttered Skye. She was trying to shrink back against the wall at her back. To disappear. "From the effulgency of light sprang reawakened energies and from the divine light emanated the forms – the Primordial Flame. I have read it. Now behold Moros, swift son of the divine sons. Behold the Charon."

Through the blood-thick mystic haze came the tortured shriek of the formless mass that writhed amongst the shadows. The mass, alien and obscene, shifted and heaved constantly, tugging at its heavy chains. A chasm of molten fire ensued. The chains of the abyss could no longer hold the Charon from fury and uproar. From beyond the Gate they came, awakened from their long slumber, locked in chains, immovable as the world forgot their ceremonies and sacrifices and ultimately forgot the Charon and their true nature. This was no single ferryman as the myths would have scholars believe, but seven merciless unholy and foul beings carrying the keys to the abyss.

A hawk-headed man appeared, looming larger than life, a prince of the underworld, with a beating black heart. He was a bringer of certain death, a terrifyingly slow and painful death, too hideous to describe, for Skye had brought forth the Charon from their slumber. Her actions formed a long forgotten arcane spell, directly manipulating mystical energies that wove and bound space and time.

He raised a wing and from the shadow it cast poured all sorts of demons and hell spawn. Hail and fire mixed with blood rained down into the study. A hellish hue prevailed as the spawning continued without end.

Imminent death most definitely stared Skye in the face. To her, this seemed like the antichrist at the breaking of the first seal. But she could just make out seven beings in total, shifting, changing, and morphing in the shadows of the thick haze. She slowly closed the book and stood up. She could feel her heart pounding so hard it almost thumped its way out of her breast. She was breathless. Her bowels felt like they would give way at any minute, but she summoned enough nervous courage to speak.

"Wh… who's there in the shadows?"

The hawk-headed man leaned forward to protrude from the hell-stuff. She could smell the stench of his breath and feel his heat upon her neck and chest. As he came closer, he changed, he was no longer hawk-headed. His face was beautiful, androgynous. His handsome face was pale, and he wore a jewelled eye-patch over his right eye. His features were fine and feminine with flame-coloured hair. Around his neck he wore a fine blue silk scarf tied in a knot at his throat. He was dressed in red, skin-tight garments through which bulged infeasibly large muscles that were at odds with his facial features. Every sinew and muscle fibre could be seen rippling beneath his clothing. He wore white stockings and simple black princely looking shoes, all of which were partly obscured by a cloak of blue.

He spoke softly. "Shadows are like doors. Doors to dark prisons…. You should never play in the shadows, you never know who… or what… may be there waiting to cross the threshold of that particular door!" He laughed a hellish evil laugh, and she felt the very ground beneath her feet shake. This was a force infinitely more powerful than anything on earth.

She was terrified. No book was worth this much. All aggression and defiance had left her. She knew this was the start of something far bigger than she or Solomon would want to entertain. All she could think of was that this must be the start of the apocalypse. Her mind raced. The Book of Revelation, that's all she could come up with. She began quoting under her breath the little she knew:

"The beast that thou sawest was, and is not; and shall ascend out of the bottomless pit, and go into perdition: and they that dwell on the earth shall wonder, whose names were not written in the book of life…" *The book of life, that must be it*, she thought. "…from the foundation of the world, when they behold the b… beast…the beast that was, and is not, and yet is."

Water welled up in her eyes. They were no longer bright and youthful. Her vision blurred. She felt her stomach quiver and her legs began to shake. Her mouth was dry. An involuntary tear rolled down her cheek and hung suspended on her chin. This moment seemed like forever, she thought, aware of her impending doom, but unaware that urine was running down her inner thigh. *Where was Ignatius?*

"You quote certain familiar verses. So, I take it, you must be the whore of Babylon?" he whispered close to her face in a hushed gruff voice, at odds with his beautiful, sweet face. "You may know me as Baal, Set or Urian, but you can call me Jack!" he laughed.

"I am Adonai, Grand Master of the Charon, Master of the Beautiful and the Damned." Without hesitating, his arms swung up and over his shoulders. He now grasped a large, wide sword, the pommel of which was carved into a death's head. Like a panther, with one seamless arc he swung the sword to cleave Skye from her shoulder, through her breastbone and down to her pelvis. Her terrified face barely comprehended what was happening.

"The End Times, have they begun….?" She gasped, almost inaudibly as she released her grasp on the book and let the cover close.

She whimpered a little and looked down as her innards spilled to the floor with a heavy wet thud. Her body slumped and fell on top of them, and a pool of blood flowed outward across the floorboards like an overflowing tub. It flowed like the flow of time, which, in contrast, had come to stand still in this gloomy study. The stench of death filled the air. There is no one who cannot afford the passage or are not admitted to the underworld by the Charon, but many who meet with a merciless dreadful death are doomed to wander the Ghost Worlds for an eternity.

Chapter 6 – The Book

Although Solomon had been an adept in the occult, the mystical and the alchemical, in reality, he knew very little, as do all men. Only seldom is one enlightened enough to understand the Truth. Even the gods have their restrictions and boundaries. For the foundations of all worlds, of all life, no matter which plane they are on, are laid by the creator of the Book of Consciousness and no other. All life forms act out a reality that is transient, a reality that is governed by the fate within the book. The body is eventually transient, just a vehicle destined for a wasteland. Only the soul lives on as an integral part of the cosmos.

Adonai took a great purposeful stride across the room, stepping over the dead bodies of Solomon and Skye, coming to rest at the Book of Consciousness – the great history of all the souls of the cosmos.

"The seal is broken", he said to the others, as he touched the book cover. He grasped the edge of the mighty book that lay before him and tried to open it, but the book remained closed. It would not open. He grasped the edge of the cover with both hands and pulled with all his might. His muscles bulged, sinews grew tighter, and veins popped out upon his neck. Even a god has his limitations depending upon which plane he has ventured, for try as he might, the book would not yield.

"This book is cursed", he exclaimed, "it will not open, 'least not for me. I cannot believe that our fate has brought us this great fortune at last and yet we are still denied any answers. The book has been closed, and we are not able to open it again, such are the paradoxes set within the cosmos, just because we may be immortal, just because we are demons, gods, not all rules apply, not all privileges; only those set by the Omnisoul at the beginning of time apply."

"What did you expect?" A woman stepped forward out of the shadows. "All the same, within the book lies our destiny," she said. "At least, we now possess Turiya, the Book of Consciousness, the akashic record of the entire cosmos as written by the First Cause, the Omniscient One, the Omnisoul. We may be the First Seven Breaths of the Omnisoul, but the secrets of our own existence have always eluded us. But at least we are closer now than ever before."

Her hair was fair, almost platinum, and shone like the sun. Her features were finely sculpted with high cheek bones and a square jaw. Her eyes were a piercing sapphire, with a gaze that would cut through any man. She was beautiful and a tall fighting figure, lean and shapely, dressed in combat leathers and a hooded black cloak. A girdle was slung low on her hips and a long broadsword, the choice weapon of a true warrior, hung low on her hips. Her legs appeared even longer, exaggerated by thigh-high black leather boots, rolled back on themselves at the top, covering her sinuous thighs, which although very feminine, showed the faint traces of battle scars.

"You are right, Tara. We know the Omnisoul would never just give up the secrets of the cosmos, the secrets of life, but we have waited for so long and now it is within our grasp we are still denied the knowledge we seek," said Adonai.

Fiercest of the female Charon, Tara cultivated fear and dread, even amongst her worshippers. Human sacrifice to her was not uncommon both in battle and conjuration; she showed no mercy in her blood lust. Her warrior priestesses seldom felt the need to summon her, for fear of the unpredictable consequences. She leaned down and touched the book's cover. The book seemed to let out a faint murmur as she did so, as if acknowledging her touch.

"We cannot risk remaining in the same place with it for long or the Omnisoul will sense the connection," said Adonai. "We will have to find a more secure plane temporarily until we have located within its sentient pages the nature of our fate and the way in which we can change it."

Another of the Charon stepped forward out of the shadows and the smoke haze that surrounded him. The smoke cleared a little as he removed the long pipe from his mouth. "Perhaps I should try?"

"Aryas, can you….?" A faint question formed on Adonai's lips.

It was just possible to make out his face a little in the gloom and the gradually disappearing smoke. His oval eyes had a mischievous twinkle in them. But one didn't want to stare into his eyes for long for fear of being trapped in some dream time with no escape.

His features were well defined, with high cheekbones, a pointy jaw and slightly pointed ears. His hair was dark like midnight and unruly, falling in clusters beneath a broad-brimmed floppy hat. Aryas was dressed like a dandy in a long deep purple coat of brocade and velvet, with a white ruffled shirt and a colourful waistcoat of midnight blue and gold thread, depicting the heavens. He was every inch the psychedelic wanderer, every inch a dreamer, a user of herbs and potions to cross each and every realm to experience to the fullness of his vast immortal life. He was a master of divination. He was always searching for new experiences, new dreams and new answers in which to take his solace. But as yet he had not found the one truth which the Charon desired.

From a little velvet bag upon his side he took out what looked like a glass pipe, replacing the pipe he was already smoking. It had a long thin curved stem swooping down to meet a large bulbous container on the end, not too dissimilar to the shape of a saxophone. He poured some green liquid into the bulb from a small, bejewelled glass vial.

Aryas walked over to the book with a swagger. He jumped up on to the tome in a sprightly fashion and sat down cross-legged upon it.

Drawing back his ruffled sleeve, he drew a secret symbol in the air with a long bony finger. He placed the glass pipe to his lips and began to ingest the liquid that was now bubbling and hissing. It moved like chaotic hell-stuff, as if imbued with a life of its own. To a human onlooker, should there have been one amongst the two corpses, it would have looked like a thick emerald-green potion containing nightmares and ghostly faces surfacing and trying to escape.

For Aryas, all time shrank from him in his state of cosmic bliss. The room in which he sat rolled up like a scroll before him as if he had filed it away somewhere for later. He had dismissed from his consciousness all thought of the earth and its course, directing his mind to the threads of the vast cosmos that now lay before him, making his mind more receptive.

Aryas's body was motionless and to the other Charon appeared on the outside no different. He began to chant quietly in some unknown language, some high speech long since forgotten. "Shaktipat, Nephesh Chiah. Sahaja. Ohm maneee arrsharoo. Ong namo gurdev namo."

Gradually his breathing became more shallow, almost undetectable, and Aryas could feel his body growing colder and colder almost like a breeze of cool vibrations running through his entire body. The sensory perception within his fingertips became heightened and Aryas was able to feel the flow of energy rising up from the base of his spine and feel the life force of the cosmos itself. He saw the courses of the luminaries in the heavens and passed by each of them, understanding their relationship to each other and their place within the creation. The intensity within his body grew and his consciousness concentrated on a single brilliant white light that burned within the root of his third eye, his spiritual eye. Transcending the limits of individualised consciousness, his spiritual self-transformation was complete.

Aryas was barely visible to the others in the cavern, just a mass of cosmic dust looking like some kind of stellar field. He had surfaced through a portal on the astral plane. Before him was a vision so clear he could smell it, touch it. After some time exploring these astral planes, Aryas came out of his meditation and slowly reappeared before the rest of the Charon. Placing one hand on each knee, he closed his eyes and spoke. "I cannot open it, but there is something about this whole coincidence that doesn't seem quite right," he said. He looked sceptical.

"We are called back to this place, to this primitive sphere after nearly two thousand years and by a means not used since then; and when we arrive, laying there before us is our heart's desire. The very means by which we can understand and end our own immortal suffering," he scowled. "It seems too easy."

"Plus, I know that I am the one gifted with a view further across the planes of existence than the rest of you, but have you not felt it? The faint pull, the attraction to yet another plane? Yet another mission. We wait for an eternity and then are called twice in quick succession… The Ti-Botta are calling, no less."

Aryas looked around at the other six members of the Charon, now shifting out of the shadows. Their eyes met and were full of sorrow and helplessness, the hope they initially bore upon seeing the great book now gone, for they knew he spoke the truth.

"The incantations will be gathering impetus even as we speak, and the Omnisoul will soon feel our efforts. We must be gone from here quickly. I suggest we set about securing our prize now, before it is too late," he said.

"But it does raise the question, how did the human open it? How is it possible for her to have the gift?" said Adonai.

"A minion" suggested Devi. "She must be a minion, offspring of Calabi-Ya, which means he must be on his way." The female aspect of the divine and the sacred force, Devi was the most dynamic embodiment of the primordial cosmic energy and dynamic forces that move through the entire cosmos. Counterpart of Adonai, she was tall, lithe and dressed in a red leather corset and red leather thigh-length boots; a formidable figure, long limbed and supple in her movements, like a big cat. Her stature reflected an unusual strength and her gaze captivated mortal men. Her eyes were dark molten pools that fixated them. Her full red lips could smile a comforting smile whilst, without blinking, she could rip a man's heart out. Her full womanly figure gave no hint of the awful mercilessness nature of this red terror. Her unruly raven long hair lay tussled about her face. She was divinely beautiful. At least her bodily adornment on this plane was.

"Did you not see through her in your haste, Adonai? I have considered her soul, and she carries the mark. I am certain her ancestry is that of Calabi-Ya. In some distant past, an ancestor had been visited by a Nephilim, a demon of the Elder God, Calabi-Ya. She must be some stealth-like means to help Calabi-Ya enter this world to search for the book for his own means. Her ignorance would be the only reason she may have opened the book."

"But surely Calabi-Ya is still in exile? If he isn't and descends upon us, this world will not survive!" said Adonai. He looked at the grizzly corpse lying on the floor. "Then she also had need of the book for herself and for Calabi-Ya, but how can she have the gift to be able to open it? Anyone with a vested interested is prohibited. Are his Nephilim that powerful, now? Perhaps the Omnisoul still toys with us. Unless, of course, she didn't know her true ancestry and therefore remained innocent?"

"Of course, she could always know how to separate herself from the Maya – the purely limited physical and mental reality. And so could achieve the opening of the book. I guess we will never know now," said Aryas.

"Then we must leave this plane now until we have a plan and see why we are being called again by the Ti-Botta and see what other mission we have been set," said Adonai.

Chapter 7 – The Dawning

Outside of Solomon's house, Ignatius and Indigo tentatively hid in the shadows at the end of the crescent, unsure whether they should have trusted Skye, an outsider. As they hid trying not to even breathe lest they draw attention to themselves, they heard the silent night air split suddenly with the crack of a steam pistol being fired.

"Oh no!" exclaimed Ignatius, "What has she done? This was never going to be easy, but this…?"

"It could be Solomon. She could be injured," said Indigo.

"No… I don't think so. Skye is a risk we should never have taken. Too volatile, unpredictable"

Suddenly a bright brass drone flew past just above their heads, escaping from Solomon's house, leaving a steamy vapour trail across the night sky.

"Drone!" he whispered and made to grab it, but it had gone.

"Now what do we do?" enquired Indigo. She was answered, but not by Ignatius. A great steam walker rounded the end of the street, clanking towards them at full speed and visibly adorned with the markings of the Administorium. Inside the mechanical beasts, the two Union agents knew, were several Administrators, each of which were part interrogator, part assassin, part fanatical warrior priest, part engineer, part lawman, part judge and all-round executioner. A full-scale battle with the Administorium was not what they had in mind. This was meant to be a clean simple mission, carried out in complete ignorance, or so they thought, by a complete unknown with no links back to the Union. Solomon was a feeble academic. How could things have gone so terribly wrong?

As Ignatius and Indigo pushed further back into the shadows, they carefully reached for their weapons. It was a good job they had come prepared; a Derringer would have been no good in this situation. Out of his engineer's waistcoat, Ignatius pulled a steam cannon. He looked over at Indigo, trying to make out the expression on her face, which was hidden in the shadows. Indigo, meanwhile, fumbled amongst her petticoats and drew out the same.

The clanking of the great steam monolith as it thundered down the road was going to awaken the whole neighbourhood, making it impossible for the two of them to escape. Suddenly, Ignatius broke out into a sweat. At least, that was what he thought. He became breathless and his vision blurred. His body felt wet, as if a cold sweat had gripped him. He held his head in his hands as his body contorted. Crimson visions of bloody Hell ran through his mind, death and destruction and a scene of Skye's twisted features appeared as if he was there in the room with her. He could even smell the stench of death and burning flesh as he watched the banquet of doom before him.

"What's wrong?" whispered Indigo, "what is it?" She watched his body became more and more distressed and contorted. *Was it pain? What was happening?*

His vision continued. Ignatius could not answer Indigo as his body was possessed by the bizarre situation. He could feel his body vibrating involuntarily, though he could hear the very cosmos screaming in anger. As he took his hands away from his face, his vision cleared, and he could see his hands were stained red, red with the blood of Skye's death. The birth mark on his right hand began to burn more than ever before. He was wet with gore, but how could this be?

As he looked up, Indigo was retching, trying not to run away, holding onto her bodily functions as best she could, backing away from her co-agent in horror. "What the....!"

All thoughts of the great clanking walker heading their way had vanished. The words hardly forming in her dry throat, she thought she was going to choke; all moisture had drained from her throat as her body went limp. She backed further away in sheer horror. All stealth was about to be given up as she gurgled enough voice to scream. But the scream never came, and the two of them were wrapped in deepest darkness like the velvety wings of the Grim Reaper himself, suffocating the very life from their sorrowful convulsing bodies, the great brass walker completely forgotten about.

Then, suddenly, the veil of darkness was lifted from their eyes and Ignatius's attire was completely clean once more. The two friends were now standing beside the lifeless body of their minion in Solomon's study. Skye's body was reflected in a pool of blood; there was so much of it she appeared to be floating on it.

Ignatius stood a little uneasily, a cavernous feeling growing in his stomach. How did they get here? He lifted his eyes slowly from the gory sight on the floor. The Great Book lit his face with a green eerie glow. Unaware of anything else in the room, he touched it, and it seemed to hum, as if trying to speak to him. He took a nervous grasp of the emerald book cover, but nothing moved. He looked at Indigo. Stepping forward, she ran her delicate fingers along the edge of the book and it started to sing. She tentatively lifted the cover by the corner but got no further than a few inches. Electrical charge encircled her arm, crackling and shooting through her whole body. Her entire body reflected the green glow of the book. She opened the cover and blinding whiteness filled her vision and she felt her body become weightless as if having an out-of-body experience. Her senses were all heightened, and she lost herself in a world of some higher being's making. She drifted at first in a silent void of white light, her body being pulled apart atom by atom, stretching over an eternity.

Although the book was open, Indigo had to fight with all of her might to keep it that way. She could feel the cover trying to close, to hide its secrets, until at last the book triumphed in the encounter and it snapped shut once more. Indigo fell into a crumpled heap on the floor, exhausted by her efforts. Ignatius clutched her in his arms, comforting her. Although the two had worked closely together for a few years, purely professional, they had developed a familiar bond between them and would do anything for each other. Ignatius brushed her hair back from her face, concerned his partner had been too badly injured in some way. Gradually, when Indigo had regained some strength, the two comrades eventually became aware of shadows surrounding them, watching them. Ignatius lifted his head. There before him stood seven beings, the like of which he had never seen before. It was almost like being at the theatre, he thought, looking at their attire.

The being before him, which he took to be a man, was dressed in a bright red outfit that betrayed the owner's muscular build; and although Ignatius had never seen him before, he thought that he was somehow familiar. Reports of Spring-Heeled Jack had commented on scarlet clothing and a blue cape.

Momentarily, Adonai paused to take in the overall scene. It had been a long time since anyone had summoned the Charon to Earth. Here before him were four mortals, two dead and two who seemed somehow different, more intelligent and sharper than most. It wasn't very often a god became confused, if confusion is what this was. Adonai uncharacteristically hesitated. But what was overwhelming was the steady green glow that bathed them all emanating from the book. At the realisation of the situation, the immortal's one visible eye seemed to widen and glint.

"Forgive our intrusion" he spoke softly, in keeping with his facial features, but at odds with his muscular bulk. "My name is Adonai and although we have many names, we are the Charon. We wish you no harm since you did not call directly upon us or indeed ever worship us, for I am a prince of darkness and such worship can be costly."

He gave a sinister grin and Ignatius knew he was probably lying about how much danger they were in. "And you are…..?"

Ignatius stood taught and confident, "I am Ignatius, and this is Indigo."

"Very well. I am curious as to how you and your deceased friend are able to open the Great Book." He looked at Indigo. "There are only two types of being with such power – those who have no vested interest in the contents contained within the artefact, completely ignorant of its contents, of its worth, a rare being indeed; and those born of the Elder God! So, which are you? I think I know, but I guess the real truth remains to be seen."

Ignatius and Indigo were speechless and pale. They weren't sure what to say. This was the very book they sought. Their journey had begun two years earlier, knowing that there was a book that could bring harm to the Empire, but they didn't know how. The plan was to secure the book and take the investigation from there. They had no idea this is what they were getting into.

"What do you mean, Elder God?" Ignatius asked nervously. "Elder God? Gods? We just wanted the book to secure it so it was of no danger to the Empire"

"Ah, well. I don't know why I should tell you this, but the book contains our fate, and we want to know it. The last time we tried to find out what fate this terrible cosmos has in store for us, I lost the sight of an eye." His remarkable bejewelled, metallic eyepatch over his right eye glinted in the darkness as he laughed, an ominous dark laugh that filled the air with his malevolence.

Adonai's nature to destroy the two humans was inhibited. He found them curious beings and he knew the Charon probably had need of them at the moment, and so he began to explain. "The Charon are seven immortal beings, playing out our fate across the thirty-one planes of existence. In what form we are perceived may vary from plane to plane, but often mimicking the life forms of the planet upon which we have descended. Our…."

He didn't have time to finish. Suddenly, and without warning, a brilliant white blast tore through the side wall of Solomon's study. Brick and plaster were pulverised into a fine dust and rolled throughout the room, obscuring the view and adding to the dimness. Even Adonai and the rest of the Charon were taken by surprise and knocked off balance momentarily. Aryas was immediately back in the cavern. The loud clanking of brass and gears came tearing through the smoking hole left in the wall of Solomon's study. Not one but two Administorium walkers came crunching through the debris. The hissing of steam and whirring of gears could be heard as pistons and hydraulics did their job and carried the occupants with ease, searching for the two Union Jacks agents.

As the machines advanced, the gleaming brass and steel glowed green in the light of the emerald book. These were machines to be dreaded. If the Administorium had a task to do, these were sent in before the Ecclesiarchy to clear the way of any immediate danger. Ignatius and Indigo knew they only had a certain amount of time before the place would be teeming with the Administorium.

Indigo had been knocked off her feet by the blast. "I wonder how much they know?" whispered Ignatius helping her to her feet. "Are you alright?"

"I'm fine, but what are we dealing with here? Gods?"

"Indigo, I have no idea, but we are going to have to run with it. I have a feeling everything we thought we knew is about to be turned on its head."

They both watched as the beautiful androgynous face of Adonai contorted with rage. He raised his arms and grabbed his enormous wide-bladed sword from his back. Every sinew and vein on his chest and arms popped and stretched like steel cable. As he lunged forward to swing, he called "Paladin, some assistance please."

Another one of the Charon stepped forward out of the shadows. His face was rugged and well worn, battle scarred. To look into his eyes was to stare death in the face. He was a knight dressed in ornate, antique-looking bronze-coloured armour. The breastplate was emblazoned with an ornate dragon, around which were carved ancient runic-like symbols. Swinging from his hips was a heavy chain belt, from which hung a colourful apron with more mystical designs and a reliquary containing consecrated scrolls and a war icon. His cloak of royal purple wrapped around his thick-set battle-worn body. His massive arms carried a mighty master-crafted weapon that was part halberd and part what looked like a musical instrument. Upon his back, he carried a huge book of spells so powerful their use was limited to battles on the higher planes, for their use might initiate spawning and demonic events beyond the control of the Charon, events with devastating consequences – more vile and powerful, than may be listed here.

The warrior god was simply named after his profession. He looked like a holy swordsman, skilled in all aspects of war, a massive formidable sight in his huge armour, which increased his strength ten-fold, making him the most powerful among the Charon.

He lunged forward, crushing the lifeless body of Solomon beneath his armoured foot. He was much quicker and nimbler than the walkers and had already swung into a fighting stance before the lead walker had its steam cannons ready. Ignatius could just make out the look of fear on the pilot's face inside the walker as Paladin swept his weapon in a large arc, cutting cleanly through one of the legs of the walker. Steam hissed from several broken pipes and hydraulic fluid leaked out like black blood, dribbling onto the floor of the study. The walker twitched and leaned to one side. The keen blade sliced the air in several more arcs as the walkers retaliated, letting loose some cannon fire that blew large holes in the book cases and walls of Solomon's house. Ignatius and Indigo had to dive this way and that to avoid the chaos that ensued. Then Paladin steadied his weapon and, placing a nozzle to his mouth, blew a devastating wave of vibrations, the sound waves emanating in a sonic blast that took out all the controls on both the walkers and then shattered the machines into thousands of tiny pieces. Ignatius and Indigo felt the sonic blast almost cave their chests in; the sound seemed to make the very fabric of space reverberate; the very fabric of the building around them seemed to warp and shift as if made from a liquid and then returned to its usual rigidity. The fight was over. Ignatius and Indigo crouched behind broken wall debris; their mouths wide open with astonishment. No one had ever dealt with a walker so efficiently, let alone two.

As quick as lightning, a drone flew in through the hole in the wall, recording all that could be observed, its tiny wings flapping and hissing steam as it darted unpredictably this way then that to avoid capture or attack. As quickly as it had appeared it vanished, to report back to the Administorium.

"They will send more" said Ignatius, "I think we may all need to be somewhere else."

"Then we will destroy them, we will destroy this entire planet if we have to!" snarled Adonai with rage. "You mere humans have the ability to open this book, so you are coming with us. You have your uses. Come, we should leave here." He gestured towards Ignatius and Indigo and then they were all gone, somehow spirited away as if by magic.

Chapter 8 – The Mystical City

A bloody globe hung amidst a pale purple sky. At first glance, the desolate, frozen waste below appeared to be completely devoid of any life. Myriad shapes formed from the blue mists, only to flicker and fade. Then, suddenly, the world turned crimson and the heavens turned black and there came a mighty roar of laughter, hate and frustration, and the cosmos trembled with unholy joy. A cold wind blew – a mysterious howling wind that might have come from limbo itself.

From the alien mists appeared a city. It looked unreal – sometimes it stood out sharply, sometimes it seemed about to vanish. The materials of its construction were breath-taking: black marble veined with red, blue and purple; orange marble veined with black; white marble veined with yellow – an entire spectrum of colours. Its huge pillars were of onyx and obsidian, its slender towers faced with gold. Quartz, ruby and emerald lay in abundance. This was the marvelled city of Sagharta, inhabited by a lost race whose science and technology was far in advance to the rest of the planet. It was said the Sagharta had escaped surface cataclysms by their multi-planed dwelling.

The city was built with monolithic wind harps on its upper arches, which moaned loudly in the chill wind, striking fear into anyone who should ever find the city. Dotted around were smaller temples marked by prayer flags, the only movement that indicated signs of life. As they approached, it became apparent just how huge the great edifice really was. The Administorium would have been dwarfed in comparison. The entire scene was extraordinarily beautiful.

The mountains lay beyond the Land of Fire and Ice, and the kingdom lay beyond the clouds. So isolated was this land that it remained locked in a sort of time capsule. The inhabitants dressed in robes of purple and gold. They were the oldest race on earth, long since forgotten, remembered in only a few obscure myths. They had become a fabled race with a fabled city of gold, a mirage upon planet earth. Mythology claimed they were the chosen race, the watchers, self-created beings to guard the Truth. Mythology had fashioned their land to be a portal to the Otherworld. The warrior monks and high priests of this sect were experts in astronomy, mathematics, physics, the occult sciences, music and art, and had mastered the art of enlightenment and could, at will, be at one with the cosmos: feel its breath, feel its heartbeat. It was difficult to tell if they resided on this world full time, part time or even at all. They were the only true masters of the Arcane Knowledge required to be in harmony with the cosmos.

This was a mysterious kingdom, lost within the mists of a hidden valley. The golden roofs and towering rainbow-coloured parapets were dwarfed only by the snow-capped mountain range that surrounded this majestic city residing at the centre of the tranquil Lake of the Celestial Lotus.

The city was fabulous; it appeared to be floating on the frozen lake, its construction growing out of what looked like a giant lotus flower. Its slender towers soared high above the frozen wastes, piercing the sky like some gothic edifice. It was impossible to determine a portal through which to enter, but its great central arch boasted what looked like two colossal wind pipes. More pipes could be seen elsewhere upon the surface of the citadel. To either side of the central arching pipes lay an oversize wind harp that moaned constantly as the wind gently blew across the strings. Each harp was tuned slightly differently, so that together they complemented each other in harmony; a harmony that mystically played out ambient music across all the planes of existence, causing perhaps, effects similar to that of the butterfly effect, but on a cosmic scale.

Beneath the wind harps was an immense prayer wheel whose technology meant it was automatically turned by the lightest breeze. Atop the towers, here and there, burned the odd fire stack, depositing a warm glow into the chill atmosphere. Strips of coloured cloth printed with prayers were strung across the tops of the towers and fluttered in the wind, purifying the air.

The jagged mountains ran around the city in an arc, protecting the valley. This was the remnants of a giant impact crater formed in the ancient past. The fabulous city was built on the central peak of the crater, which was called Kaylasa. Out of what was once a dead wasteland blossomed the city like a lotus flower, well-protected from the harsh mountain winds by the outer rim of the crater. The city was a technological achievement of great sophistication.

Mythology had fuelled the stories that this land was a vast subterranean world reached only by a twisting network of tunnels leading down from secluded arcane temples. The entrances were indicated by secret signs and symbology. Travellers to this region heard stories of hidden entrances guarded by monsters and acolytes whose secret duties were an ancient tradition handed down to the initiated through the millennia.

The Ti-Botta race consisted of a caste of warrior monks and high-priests, a proud noble people with ancient traditions and a well-developed spiritual canon. The true history of these people was known only to an elite circle of high priests, who had passed through all stages of a secret initiation. They were experts in the magic arts, having been granted the gift by the Seven Sublime Lords, the Charon. Among their many secrets was the claim that gods had been born among them.

Great sky galleons hung in the air, tethered to landing platforms atop the tallest towers. They were magnificent airships with ornate colourful hulls and huge striped sails, golden-carved bows and ship's quarters as big as a palace. Great balloons of gas filled the sky, strapped to the galleons by nets and cables as thick as a man's thigh.

The Ti-Botta people, ancient and mysterious, a mere myth to most people; but real enough to those who knew how to find them. These were few as the Land of Fire and Ice resided at a gateway between worlds, a weakness in the aether and, at times, the great city faded in and out of view, or even existence; the catastrophe wrought by the impact that had struck the earth during pre-history had ruptured the fabric of the cosmos, making it weak and at times penetrable.

They knew the effect the Dark Arts had on the very fabric of the cosmos. The fabric becomes weak, creating bridges across the great divide to the Ghost Worlds and Demon Worlds, allowing for that which is unmanifest upon this plane to become manifest. The Ti-Botta didn't need to see the wings of death that now cast their shadow across the globe, they had felt the Timequake caused by the actions of Ragnar of Roc as the resultant events ripped across the meticulously woven threads of the spacetime fabric like ripples in a pool caused when a stone falls into it.

In the nave sat the priests. All were male and each was rotating an ornate prayer wheel. A continuous droning hum, chanting filled the void. Their resonances echoed around the taut upright structure of the temple. The walls reverberated like the tight strings of an instrument. The vibrations caused an atmosphere that seemed to heighten the senses.

On either side of the great altar was a huge cylindrical prayer wheel, each twice the height of a man, each being rotated by a slender naked woman, their dark sweating bodies glistening in the torch light. Upon the altar sat a wizened old man with a long white beard. In front of him, a large singing bowl the diameter of an oil drum and around its rim his skeletal hand ran a pestle around and around until the noise ringing out from it threatened to destroy the very walls surrounding them all.

Behind the old man who, by his clothes and head dress must have been the High Priest, was a giant of a man. He was young and full of rippling muscles, evident due to his nakedness. As the chanting and metallic singing came to a crescendo the giant picked up a mallet and crashed it singularly with the force of a speeding steam gurney into the hide of a gargantuan drum. The thunderous beat would have deafened a lesser being. The sound waves travelled out through the temple walls like a sonic boom, out across several dimensions until they reached the Charon. They had been called for a second time.

Although most of the modern world no longer know the Charon, for this one small, isolated sect, drifting in and out of time, across planes and sometimes appearing high in the bleak mountains of the northeast, hidden from the rest of civilisation, the Charon would never be forgotten. It was said that when no person worships a particular deity, that god ceases to exist. If the

Charon could kill every being in every world on every plane that knew of their existence, or worshipped them, or had even read about them in some ancient tome, they would. That's why they were so cruel to those they met. They cared not to be remembered, for it was said that immortality cannot trouble the non-existent. But for the Charon, there was no such fate, for them this task had seemed fruitless despite their best efforts.

When the chanting had stopped, the vibrations of the drum and singing bowl had stopped and the incantation complete, the mighty temple lay silent. Not even the wildlife outside stirred. The High Priest of the Ti-Botta people sat cross-legged upon his dais on the altar. The Ti-Botta race had no king or queen; they were an entirely ecclesiastical race with the High Priest their Grand Master. Different Chapters were devoted to each of the seven Charon and were all present in the temple.

Slowly, a dark writhing mass began to form above the altar. Despite being used to the calling, the High Priest couldn't help but let out a faint gasp at first sight. Quite sure none of his brothers had seen or heard, he re-gathered his stately composure when the mass had finally descended, and then before the High Priest stood a vision of the seven Charon and two humans. Curiously, thought the High Priest, Paladin stood with a great emerald coloured tome tied to his back, the magic runes carved on his ancient bronze armour glowing green.

"My Lord, your presence is humbly requested," said the High Priest in a quiet voice, his eyes lowered to the floor.

Atman stepped forward in front of Paladin. He had platinum blond hair, shoulder length and swept to one side. He was pale with a good bone structure, sunken cheeks, and fine features. His eyes were cold – steely powder blue, the same as his cloak. His eyes reflected very much his nature, quiet calm and extremely cold with no mercy in his heart. He was the quietest of the Charon and his melancholy nature did not bode well with the others. He wore a black leather jerkin, pale blue pantaloons with white stockings and simple delicate black shoes. Due to his nature, Atman was best suited talking to those who worshipped the Charon. As he did so, Adonai leaned forward and whispered in his ear "When we get there, perhaps we should just kill them all and receive the demise we are all waiting for." He gave a sinister grin, but he knew this was not possible; a god is cruelly somehow duty-bound to his worshippers.

Atman gave the High Priest the respect he deserved before his brethren. "We shall arrive soon. Then you can tell us why we have been summoned."

The vision before the altar then shifted and faded gradually until the High Priest stood alone once more.

Chapter 9 – The Ship

Ignatius and Indigo had no idea how they'd gotten to their present location. They stood upon the foredeck of the great ship Taraka. It was like a cross between an ironclad and a dirigible. Carvings covered its entire surface. It was a huge edifice, like a cross between a gothic cathedral and Art Nouveau organic forms, with magnificent arched stained-glass windows spires towering a hundred feet above. Ornate facades, flying buttresses and ornamental arches covered the entire length of the great leviathan. It looked both spiritual and hell-wrought at the same time, with parts of the hull either rusty or encrusted with dried blood. It was hard to tell which.

But this ship did not float upon the ocean waves, although it was likely able to do so. It ploughed an invisible furrow through the cosmic ocean and the seas of time. Strangely, great clouds of what looked like steam billowed from the ship's stacks. Ignatius considered the possibility. Did the gods really travel using steam? He was sceptical; he thought to himself that this couldn't be true.

Adonai stood at the helm, his billowing blue cloak covering his rich red clothing. Ignatius thought that his face looked somewhat strained and anxious. An unexpected twist, he thought, given that he was in the presence of some kind of god. Perhaps gods were just the same, with senses, emotions, and anxieties. Perhaps all humans are indeed made in their image. Ignatius felt uneasy, though. The concept did not sit easily with him. Gods were supposed to be gods, invulnerable, masters of all.

Indigo remained close to Ignatius. Although she was made of stern stuff, as all agents had to be, he could feel her trembling a little. This whole adventure was way beyond their previous experiences. He wanted to put his arm around her for reassurance, but for some reason, he couldn't bring himself to do so. In truth, Ignatius felt completely and utterly at a loss what to do. The Union had never discussed such events. True, they had been involved with some occult activity and clandestine operations throughout their entire history, but to be involved with higher beings and events of cosmic proportions was entirely incomprehensible.

The ship ploughed on through the aether, its crew unhindered and unaffected by the lack of oxygen. Ignatius was unsure whether it was his imagination, but he thought that the ship bobbed slightly, as if it moved through water. Perhaps this was an effect of the aether. Ignatius knew that scientists had speculated that the entire cosmos was bound together with some kind of medium or vital life-sustaining force. As he glanced over the side of the ship, he could see stars flashing by, whole galaxies in the distance, gaseous nebulae came and went and whole planets drifted by at speed. They were experiencing the cosmos in the blink of an eye.

"Where are we going?" whispered Indigo. Ignatius just shrugged slightly; he didn't know any more than she did. What was most concerning was the fact that they might be the key, the only access the Charon had to the Book of Consciousness. As long as the

Charon needed access, Ignatius and Indigo still had a future, but after that, things looked bleak. Perhaps this was their fate, to die on a lonely planet somewhere else in the cosmos, not even able to leave behind a blackened smudge upon the surface of planet earth. But what saddened his patriotic heart most was the fact that he had failed the Empire.

Another of the Charon silently approached them and introduced herself. "I am Darshan. What do we call you?" She was tall and lithe, dressed in a white tunic shirt and red leather waistcoat, a large scimitar hanging at her hip.

Ignatius took the lead and, courteously trying to smile, said "I am Ignatius, and this is my colleague Indigo."

"You must have many questions. The Charon are not used to exchange, we tend to act first. Not many try and resist when they realise who we are or what the consequences will be for certain. But I sense you two are different, special in some way. I know Adonai thinks so."

"How do we sail?" asked Indigo. "It feels like we are at sea, but there is no water. How do we even breathe?"

"We sail on the cosmic breath that is present, both in and surrounding all things. You would call it the aether. We breathe due to supernatural means, although the aether isn't a vacuum anyway. It consists of all sorts of unseen energy forces, unseen matter and is a result of the fabric of space and time."

"The ships stacks, are they great clouds of steam?"

Darshan gave a faint laugh. "We burn the souls of the dead, at least those that have been judged" she said looking slightly amused, "for we are the ferry man!"

This last statement sent a shiver down Ignatius' back and Indigo felt uneasy at the thought of burning souls, her stomach churning at such a ghoulish notion.

"The dead are ferried to the underworld, as in your mythologies found on planet earth, but the souls are burned during the journey. The debris feeds the aether and keeps the cosmos fed with renewable energy. The cosmos is alive, a living organism where all our actions have an effect on another part of the cosmos. These actions cause vibrations in the fabric of space and time. The cosmos is a living, seething mass of vibrating consciousness."

"But what happens when man has become extinct, and no longer walks the earth? There will be no one to ferry. No souls to burn. What will become of you and your purpose then?" asked Ignatius.

"You assume we rely on man. You assume we are inextricably linked to the earth. We are the first seven beings brought into existence by the consciousness of the Hypersphere, we are connected to all worlds, throughout the cosmos" replied Darshan.

"The Hypersphere?" queried Indigo.

"I forget, humans are so primitive. The Hypersphere is the whole of the cosmos. There are many universes, many planes each with their own worlds. The universe you inhabit is just one small part of the Hypersphere," answered Darshan. "It is the overall encompassing entirety that is the cosmos. The central shell contains your universe and other, unique, and sometimes parallel universes, all making what is known as the Multiverse. Linking these universes are the Astral Planes that cross and entangle the planes of existence. The Shadow Worlds inhabit the Astral Planes.

Towards the outer regions of the cosmic shell are the Netherworlds, the oldest worlds that have drifted outwards due to the constant expansion. Although little is known about some of these worlds.

Outside of the cosmic shell is Limbo, the forgotten thoughts of the Omnisoul. This is inhabited by the Ghost Worlds. Nothing else exists outside of the Hypersphere."

Ignatius and Indigo were speechless.

"The Hypersphere is far more complex than humans will ever understand. Just observing your universe summons it into existence, giving it the structure and properties you observe. Perhaps what you experience is just a figment of your imagination. You will never be sure. The story of the cosmos has been laid down by one being only, the Omnisoul. The Hypersphere is the consciousness of the Omnisoul. Your lives, your experiences, have been laid down since the start of time by the Omnisoul. You have no real free-will, you exist for the amusement of the Omnisoul."

"So, our thoughts are not our own? Then why are we here? Why do we do what we do daily?" asked Ignatius with a wrinkled, puzzled brow.

"That, even the Charon cannot answer. We are all playthings of the Omnisoul. We may have some influence on our own free-will somehow, but our fates are set and sealed. It has been since the beginning of time. But when the Charon are released from time to time from our Limbo, time is no obstacle: the great ship Taraka sails the Hypersphere, between the worlds, between the planes, and we have our chance to influence our own fate."

Darshan could see the shoulders of Ignatius and Indigo clearly slump. *Humans are so helpless, feeble,* she thought. "There must be much that you do not understand. But all will become apparent. We have a long journey ahead of us, so we have time to explain some of what perhaps is troubling you."

Much to Ignatius' dismay, Indigo scowled at her defiantly and was about to lash out verbally. He quickly managed to put his arm through hers and manoeuvre her away. "Are you trying' to get us killed? Besides, who is the Omnisoul? We need to find out."

Darshan gave a faint laugh. Following the two of them, her presence seemed to grow, and she leaned forward and in a low voice spoke. "You will be safe; to extinguish you would serve us no purpose. For the first time in aeons, the Charon have within their grasp their ultimate goal. But you are at risk from others who will want to separate you from us; therefore, you have no choice but to be under our protection."

Neither Ignatius nor Indigo questioned any further for now, they just looked at each other, their blank expressions explaining more than words ever could. They had no idea what quest or misadventure they had gotten themselves into. And for now, despite being the best the Union Jacks had to offer, neither of them wanted to know.

The ship sailed on through a cloud of gaseous nebulae. Colours of deep orange burned alongside turquoise and purple. Cosmic lightning thrilled through the gas and sparked its way across light years like a fiery dragon, heating and binding together the elements that would eventually become planetary systems and, ultimately, life. The clouds of excited electrons buffeted the ship, which swayed occasionally from side to side, its hull starting to warm up in the magnetic storm that gathered and swirled about her. It was like travelling through the aurora borealis, thought Ignatius. As they entered further into the cloud of gas, the bow of the ship began to glow hot. Everyone on deck had to brace themselves against the fiery whirlwind, covering their faces with their great coats and cloaks against the searing burning gas.

Although uneasy, Indigo had mellowed towards Darshan. "Where are you taking us?" she asked quietly for fear her voice might echo across the cosmos through which they travelled.

"Come", said Darshan in a cheerier note, "let us go below deck and get more comfortable, and I will explain a little." She turned and strode away, her long limbs carrying her quickly, heading for below deck.

In one of the lower cabins, Darshan sat in the gloom, her beautiful face partially lit by a lamp, her dark ringlet hair forming a halo around her head. Ignatius and Indigo sat at the great oak table opposite her.

"Where are we going to?" asked Ignatius nervously.

"We are heading to the fabled city of Sagharta in the land of the Ti-Botta. The Ti-Botta are ancient priest-like warriors, the heralds of the Charon upon the earth, but a different earth to that you are accustomed to. They are practitioners of esoteric practices and masters of consciousness, which explains the most repeated symbol in their land – the all-seeing eyes of the Ti-Botta. They are capable of summoning the Charon; and we have been summoned!

"The Ti-Botta live upon the earth in the Land of Fire and Ice. It is a strange mystical land that exists across more than one plane and therefore cannot be found easily, sometimes fading in and out of the planes it crosses. Sometimes it exists on your present-day earth and at times on an alternative earth. Due to the ghostly property of the kingdom, and the fragility of the planes it crosses, the land is fissured with deep crevasses where molten lava flows forth from the earth, giving it the name the Land of Fire and Ice."

"The land is surrounded and protected by a ring of snow-capped mountain peaks that are the remnants of a meteorite crater. On the central peak, the Ti-Botta built the great mystical city of Sagharta, a cathedral like edifice soaring high into the sky. Surrounding the city is the Lake of the Celestial Lotus, into which runs the River of Woe. It is said the River of Woe links the earth with the underworld, where the Charon dwell."

"For now, that is all you need to know. You should get some rest and refresh yourselves, we have a long and dangerous journey ahead of us."

With a wave of her hand, drink and food aplenty appeared upon the table. Darshan got up and left, disappearing feline-like into the gloom.

After a moment, Ignatius headed for the cabin door. "Come on, we need to get out of here."

Indigo quickly followed suit. Silently they crept along the corridor towards a staircase.

"You really should get some rest." The two agents were startled. Turning around they saw Darshan standing in the corridor. "We are hurtling through time and space. Where are you going to go? Relax. Get some rest." The two Union Jacks returned to their cabin as Darshan turned and disappeared into the gloom.

The ship continued onwards, traversing great distances and breath-taking scenes, the like of which no telescope on earth would ever experience. Colours flashed and moved as if alive, gas clouds began to clump around liquid iron balls, spinning furiously, indicating the start of new solar systems. On occasions the ship would pass through the atmosphere of strange alien worlds. Planets with yellow or pink skies, twin suns, lands of multi-coloured hues, some of which had no equivalent colour upon the earth. Oceans of brightly coloured living liquid swept along tranquil shores of turquoise sands. The mosaic of colours was too much to take in. Adonai still stood at the bow of the ship, staring out across the cosmos, as if looking for something. The ship continued eerily and steadily forever onwards, moving somehow without a crew. Occasionally the ship would cross the Ghost Planes and find itself travelling through a strange dead landscape and then find itself on a known plane, sometimes in the future, sometimes in the distant past. The ship would sometimes pass unnoticed and at other times be in full view of other beings who would sometimes attack, but to no avail; or on occasions they would begin to worship the quickly fading vision before them.

Having eaten, Ignatius said, "We should get some rest." And with that, the two of them found a corner of the room and huddled together for reassurance and comfort.

They did not know how long they slept, but they were awakened by Darshan. "We are here. The Land of the Ti-Botta. Come on deck and see."

Chapter 10 – Signs

Ignatius and Indigo followed Darshan. As they stood on deck it was cold and bright; the light was piercing. All around them were snow-capped mountains as the great ship sailed through the atmosphere of whatever planet they were on. Ignatius and Indigo peered through squinted eyes but could not make out any city in the whiteness of the mountains below.

Eventually the ship stopped, and as they disembarked a huge citadel came into view. "It's breath-taking," said Indigo.

The towers and spires soared above them, glinting in the cold sunlight. The gentle hum of the wind harps filled their ears. The two Union Jacks followed the Charon in through the great ornate portico. Indigo glanced up; the double doors must have been forty feet tall. Once inside, they were led through a marble entrance hall big enough to engulf about a third of St George's College back in Oxford. Passing through another huge doorway they all entered the Great Temple.

It was a tremendous, monumental edifice of unparalleled splendour soaring high into the air. Its repeat of high arches was a loftiness Ignatius had not seen anywhere on the earth. It looked almost supernatural. Every arch and vaulted span utilised the thrust and counterthrust of the design, resulting in perfect harmonic geometrical forces that negated each other, giving the impression of lightness, as if the building was floating instead of weighing heavily of the ornate stone used in its construction. The innovative and unusual design resulted in a temple that was capable of vibration, like an instrument made of stone. Stone that, like the fabric of the cosmos, was in a constant state of tension.

The vaults were supported at regular intervals by tall slender columns, though relatively few. Cloisters lay to the left and the right of the Great Temple and beyond these were small semi-circular chapels, each one was dedicated to one of the seven Charon.

Frescoes of the Charon adorned the dimly lit walls, telling of their labours, their adventures in the cosmos. Some were little more than horrific nightmare scenes as the Charon were depicted in various guises, not all of which were humanoid. Scattered between these chapels were further chapels that were filled with naked priestesses, their bodies glistening with oil and sweat in the candlelight.

The two Union Jacks apprehensively followed the Charon into the great temple at the heart of the city they could see warrior priests sat cross-legged upon the floor, row upon row of them, reaching into the hundreds and looking like crimson and gold clones. Incense filled the air and drifted skyward to fill the upper vaults of the great ornate edifice. Darshan turned to them and said, "This is the Unholy Order of the Lords of Damnation."

Ignatius looked at Indigo and whispered, "I'd rather not know."

Paladin removed the Book of Consciousness from its chains and several priests scurried it away, its green glow vanishing into the distance.

Indigo stayed close to Ignatius, holding his arm at times. She was courageous and had earned her place in the Union Jacks, but the images here were too alien. She glanced at the images in the semi-circular chapels to the sides, the images were too obscene for any earthling and were such that they should never been seen or experienced again.

Ignatius and Indigo stood by in the shadows trying not to be noticed. Indigo had drawn her short sword and tensed her body, ready to spring into action if required. Ignatius had his hand on the steam cannon strapped to his thigh. Atman spoke for considerable time with the High Priest, none of which either Union Jack could hear, until at length the priest spoke more openly. "The heavenly signs have shown that the great necromancer, Ragnar of Roc has opened a portal to the Ghost Worlds, and Calabi-Ya has returned. He has lain asleep for all this time, but this magic has caused a weakness in the shell of the cosmos, reawakening the great dragon. He will bring his dark energy and create an epoch of fire. Even the Charon may not be able to expel him."

Ignatius dared to ask a question of Darshan. "Who is he speaking of? What is this great threat?"

Darshan turned and replied. "Calabi-Ya. Legend has it this primordial beast existed before the creation, before the gods."

"What are the Ghost Worlds?" asked Indigo.

"Your universe is a small part of the cosmos, of what is called the Hypersphere. The Astral Planes entangle with all worlds and run parallel to them, including your universe. The Shadow Worlds exist alongside these and as you travel towards the outer regions the Netherworlds populate the cosmos, but outside of the cosmic shell exist the Ghost Worlds. These are in Limbo and consist of exiles, hellish worlds and strange beings that should never be given access to the cosmos."

Indigo looked somewhat perplexed. She looked at Ignatius, who looked equally puzzled. "The Empire pales into insignificance," said Ignatius. "I don't think the adventures of the Union Jacks has ever felt so futile."

Normally the two Union Jacks were quick on foot and nimble, a dynamic force to be reckoned with, but here they were among gods. Among other beings in the cosmos. Ignatius had fought armies, spies, even pirates who had threatened the Empire, battled with occult forces, some might even say demons and ghouls, but this was all new territory. He lowered his hand, removing it from his steam cannon. Indigo thought she saw his shoulders drop, his muscular chest slump. She realised they were helpless, outmatched for anything they were going to encounter. She put away her short sword.

After the meeting between the High Priest and the Charon came to a close, two smiling priests dressed in the usual crimson and gold shuffled towards Ignatius and Indigo and whisked them away, probably for their own safety. "Come, you must be tired. You must rest. The Charon have plans for you. Perplexed but silent, the two of them followed the priests who showed them to a small dimly lit chamber room they would be staying. They were offered refreshments and rest. Other priests came in and bowing politely they served food and tea, backing out the doorway without ever turning their back on the two Union Jacks, a kindly gesture of respect to their guests. Off to one side were two large ornate beds, fine robes, and perfumes.

Darshan had followed. "Please relax, make yourselves comfortable. You will be safe here. We will not harm you. Adonai has plans and has need of you. For the first time in eternity, the Charon have need of significant help from two humans." Then with a swish of her hips, she swung around and was gone, and the door closed behind her.

Dusk had come and the sun began to set over the black outline of the city and after a certain amount of pomp and ceremony, the Charon retired to a nearby hall with chambers running off to the one side where they secured the emerald book for further scrutiny later.

"What do you think she meant?" asked Indigo.

"I'm not sure, but we need to start understanding more about this quest. As long as they have need for us, we are safe. After that, I'm not sure. But I think we should gather our strength and be prepared for anything. We are walking with supernatural beings, with gods! Therefore, who knows what else the future holds."

Normal conversation was impossible as they ate. But they took their fill, trying to act as normal as possible. Wine had been provided, but this was different. As Ignatius drank, he could feel his body grow in warmth. He felt as if he glowed. His tired muscles felt reinvigorated and energised. "Wow! This wine's amazing!" he declared to Indigo. She smiled and scooped up her goblet. They both drank and tried to analyse what was happening, what their role would be. Ignatius knew that neither of them were being true to themselves. This is not how they would normally react, but to be in the presence of gods was a new experience. Would anyone back in Oxford, back on their earth, believe them?

"Come on, let's take a look around, we need to look for clues, any sign of our fate," said Indigo.

They headed for the door and crept along the passage, senses alert. They followed the wide corridor, retracing their footsteps Before they had reached the Great Temple, they came upon another chamber. At first glance it looked like a music room with row upon row of instruments. Indigo picked up what looked like a miniature qanun, an ancient triangular stringed instrument. Delicately she plucked at some stings, the melodic sound, although soft, seemed to vibrate through her entire body. She looked at Ignatius. "That feels strange, my whole body seemed to respond to the sound."

Ignatius picked up a similar instrument. He copied Indigo and plucked a few strings. This seemed to be a deeper resonance. Vibrations travelled up his arm and he felt like he no longer had full control over his own limb. "This is peculiar. The instruments seem to have an effect on the body like no other instrument on earth. I think we may *borrow* these; they may be useful." With that he slipped the instrument into the pocket of his engineer's waistcoat and returned to the corridor. Indigo followed suit, tucking her instrument into her petticoats.

Further on they came to some vast doors that were slightly ajar. A faint light poured out through the slit, illuminating the corridor locally. Pressing his face against the oak door, Ignatius placed an eye against the gap to gain a view of what lay inside. Indigo stooped down and followed suit.

They could see the hall was dark. The only light, although dim, came from the great arched windows that lined the west wall. The walls of the Great Hall were frescoed from floor to ceiling in red and gold, with scenes from the life of the Charon, above which was depicted one thousand Charon from the past, present and future. Hidden among the shadows sat the Charon, unmoving, their grim faces stained with the rays of the lowering sun, their eyes full of sorrow.

Ignatius could see Adonai sat staring at the single white rose he held delicately in his hand. At length he clenched it in his large fist, its crisp petals crushed. He threw it to the floor, all of its freshness and beauty destroyed. His mighty chest expanded and the silence was broken suddenly by a terrible scream. Adonai fell to his knees and began pounding the floor with both his fists. He raised his powerful body and brought his arms back. Clutching his sword, he drew it from the scabbard upon his muscular back and hurled it at an oval mirror opposite.

The mirror shattered with an almighty crash. Ignatius and Indigo were startled and instinctively pulled away from the doors. Indigo could see Ignatius had a problem with his hand; he rubbed at his birthmark as if it were causing him some irritation or pain. As they resumed their view, there were no flying shards of glass. Instead, the gleaming slivers floated eerily before busting into emerald flames. The others watching squinted. As the firelight faded and the Charon could see again, two enormous lips appeared. Ignatius and Indigo resumed their positions. The lips were iridescent blue and grinning a sinister grin. Their mocking laugh filled the hall, the city. The laughter revealed black, crooked teeth. A foul stench filled the air. Then the lips began to speak, for this was the Voice, one of the Celestials, seven powerful sorcerer lords who had obtained god-like status from an otherwise extinct civilisation in the Netherworlds. Sent by an extremely powerful warlock called the Master. In millennia past, the Celestials had waged a great war with Calabi-Ya and helped the Charon banish him. For that reason, they were favoured by the Omnisoul and given some freedom within the cosmos. Now they directed the Charon, communicating the will of the Omnisoul.

The giant pair of lips hovered and spoke. "The cosmos is in grave danger. Upon his return, Calabi-Ya has found a way to operate beyond the consciousness of the Omnisoul. He will disturb the balance of the Hypersphere, bringing chaos and entropy to whole regions of the cosmos. You must stop him. To do this, you must locate Jeeva in order to destroy him."

The lips then faded from view and the seven Charon were left looking at each other with fire in their eyes, for this is what they had been born to do, to carry out the will of the Omnisoul, but if anyone had looked carefully, they would have detected a hint of sorrow in their eyes also. For although they thrived on death and destruction, they didn't know peace of any kind, and certainly not inner peace.

Ignatius and Indigo silently retreated and raced back the way they'd come. "I'm not sure how we get out of this," whispered Indigo.

"I don't think we can. But from what Darshan tells us we are safe. At least for now. We are armed, resourceful and above all are agents of the Union. We can fight if we must. I'm not sure we will ever see Oxford again or be able to recount our tale for it to live on in the annals of our organisation's history, but as always we will remain steadfast. This is bigger than any of us; it's not just the Empire and Union at risk here, but the very fabric of time and space itself. So long as we are able to open the book when even the gods cannot, we have a usefulness to them, and with that a reason to be kept alive. And besides, at present, the Charon are paying us no attention at all. They are all lost in their own thoughts. They looked melancholy, despondent even. They look reluctant to fight."

"I wonder who Jeeva is?"

"I guess we will find out very soon," replied Ignatius with a shrug of his shoulders.

As the two of them settled in, they looked around the gloomy walls and could make out frescoes depicting the Charon in all sorts of scenes – in regal splendour, in battle or being worshipped by all sorts of other beings. Eventually they retired to bed.

Their relationship had always been strictly professional, but this evening, Indigo lay next to Ignatius for some reassurance. He placed his arm around her shoulder like a brother and the two of them fell asleep.

Chapter 11 – The Longing Desire

The following morning, flowers were strewn about the floor of the chamber and the fragrance of incense, lots of incense, pervaded the air. Candles burned upon a small dais, an offering of light to the ones who are destined to bring light.

Atman sat motionless upon the Lotus throne, exercising his mind, concentrating it with the Cosmic One. With increasing concentration, his mind became more tranquil. It grew in strength and happiness, a feeling of contentment as his mind had at last found its rightful home.

Two powder-blue eyes stared moodily from his beautiful head. His skin was ivory white and almost translucent. His angular features showed no signs of age. His platinum blond hair formed a halo around his face. Atman sat upon the throne at the far end of the Great Hall, whose high vaulted ceiling was lost in the gloom.

The slender figure sat unmoving, staring as if he looked upon some other plane. His mind drifted through the cosmos. He passed through landscapes that were beautiful and serene, across golden plains where single scarlet poppies nodded in the gentle breeze. Where yellow suns shone brightly above lush green forests of exotic fruit trees, where deep blue seas languidly washed white beaches and seabirds wheeled in the clear sky, their distant cries heard for miles. Here there was only peace.

And then the cosmos shifted, the sky began to darken. Mounted on scaly beasts appeared seven reavers, their bodies warped and twisted. From beneath their hooded, tattered cloaks shone two large orbs in which the fires of hell burned. They were inhuman and grinning. Their leader wore red with a dirty tattered blue cloak. Others were dressed in combat leather, just visible through the filth, the dried blood and dirt from aeons of battle. They were hawk-headed and three of them just discernible as female. They were hellish representations of other forms. Each of them carried a large scythe, encrusted with dried blood.

The scene became liquid, all hell tumbled and strange music, sweet and luring filled the air. The image became a mosaic of gore until the scene was torn asunder, and then was gone.

The door at the opposite end of the hall opened to reveal the lithe form of Tara with her faultless beauty and blond hair falling in rippling clusters down her supple back. Like a panther, she padded her way down the hall, unseen by Atman.

As she drew closer, Atman sat perfectly still. She came closer still, her thigh brushing against him. Her dark eyes burned beneath heavy lashes, her red lips parting as she stared into his sombre eyes. Atman was still motionless, merely raising his eyes slightly to look at her. Eventually he arched his brow, but no question formed upon his lips. For it was the same familiar question they had all asked time and time again, and for which none of the Charon knew the answer. Tara simply shook her head slowly and sympathetically.

A tear rolled down his cheek. For moments, it hung, suspended on the end of his chin, until at last, it fell to the floor to explode in a shower of white light.

At last he spoke. "Surely there must be an end, Tara? We are simply instruments on which to place the responsibilities of a higher order. Can nobody administer justice on our behalf for a change?"

He began to crack under the strain, the unbearable knowledge. He stood in a rage and Tara tried to calm him. She pressed her body against his taut form and kissed him squarely on the lips. But it was too late. He brushed her aside and drew his great battle blade. He struck the marble floor in front of him, striking it like a god gone mad until eventually it started to splinter beneath the tremendous energy released, and the whole city shook. He slumped back down upon his throne and was calm once more, drawing his legs up into a crossed position. He sat perfectly still as if alone. Tara approached him again and sat astride him upon his lap. She embraced him, their divine strength combining in the primordial union of both wisdom and compassion.

Elsewhere in the city, Ignatius and Indigo felt the city shake slightly and thought it best not to venture anywhere or enquire. For the time being they were safe.

Just then a sprightly but elderly priest entered the room to enquire if they were alright, realising the slight quake might disturb them. Ignatius thought it safe to make some enquiries.

"Forgive me," he said politely. "I think we are beginning to understand a little of who the Charon are, and a little about Calabi-Ya, but can you tell us more?"

The old man lowered his gaze and moved his head slowly from side to side. Seating himself, he spoke softly. "The cosmos is a complicated place and before you can begin to understand who Calabi-Ya is you must first understand the cosmos." He placed his hands together almost as if in prayer. He paused for a while, trying to establish the best way to explain.

"The cosmos is not what you might think."

"The academics at the Royal Society, some of which are part of the Union, believe it to be billions of years old, and infinite. Darshan explained about other worlds," said Ignatius.

"Most humans have a simple and primitive view. They fixate on the light they can see. But that light is just the surface of the cosmos. Let me show you what Darshan explained."

Pushing his sleeves up, the old man began swirling his long-fingered hands around in a circular motion whilst chanting quietly to himself in an unintelligible tongue, just audible. Tendrils of purple smoke began to form and spread out towards Ignatius and Indigo. Then turquoise sparks lit the scene as a mass of light formed into pinpoints, millions of them. Nebulous gas of all colours began to form and snake their way between the points of light, filling the void with energy. Energy that grew and pulsated.

"A map of the cosmos," gasped Indigo.

"Yes, my dear, it is merely a vision, but demonstrates the true nature of the cosmos. It is sentient and all matter is interconnected."

He waved his hands again and the cosmos split, worlds lay within worlds. "These are the planes that connect all material, all life, containing energy that vibrates and flows through us all, an energy field connecting us with no distinction between the material world and the spiritual. That energy is the Omnisoul, shaping the physical world moment by moment connected to the consciousness of all living beings."

As they looked on, the vision began to expand and grow larger. Some parts expanded more quickly than others. The whole room glowed with the myriad of colours given off by the vision.

The old man's hands began to swirl once more, his fingers held out in certain purposeful poses. "Watch."

As they did so the view began to grow, zooming in on one region of space. A cloud of gas began to form a vortex and the space around it became a turbulent storm-tossed sea until a hole opened.

"A tear in space and time. A window allowing travel between planes. This is how Calabi-Ya has been able to re-enter the cosmos. This is what Ragnar of Roc created. Capable of conversing with spirits, demons and devas, his quest for knowledge and power caused a fissure in the celestial ocean, allowing Calabi-Ya to return. Whether this act was deliberate, we do not know."

"And this Calabi-Ya, how dangerous is he?" said Indigo.

"Perhaps the most dangerous. We do not speculate on such matters for our own safety, but perhaps the Omnisoul fears him above else."

"And why would that be?" said Indigo and Ignatius in unison.

"That I cannot say." The old man paused, at which point another priest entered the room carrying an ornate golden tray upon which the two Union Jacks could instantly recognise an ornate bejewelled teapot.

"Ah, we pause for some butter tea," said the old priest, dismissing the vision so it vanished. His voice was quiet and sounded like velvet. He had a very calming effect on the two agents.

As they drank, the two could feel their bodies begin to warm. "I've never had butter tea before, but it's wonderful, very smooth and invigorating," remarked Indigo. The old man just smiled intensely, crow's feet emanating out from his eyes, his wispy white beard glinting with droplets of butter tea.

Ignatius had so many questions that he didn't know where to start. "And the Charon, how are you able to summon them? In our world it appears to be a very ancient method of placing a coin on the tongue of a dead person. Is it magic?"

The old man chuckled. "Perhaps. We send out a signal using the great sky harps, the vibrations of which travel out from our city to reach other areas of the cosmos, including Limbo. These are felt by the Keeper, who releases the Charon on their quest. The Keeper guards the Charon in Limbo. They are not left free to do as they will. Their desire is to end it all. They are immortal, and tired, but the Omnisoul would never allow it. They are used to carry out the Omnisoul's bidding when required. Any other time, they are imprisoned in Limbo."

Indigo seized her opportunity to ask, "the Omnisoul, is he God?"

"No! I mean the Omnisoul," pausing, "maybe. Something like that, but not He," came the reply with a faint smile.

"Sorry, God is a she?"

"Not She." Indigo and Ignatius looked very puzzled. Once more, the old man chuckled. "The Omnisoul is genderless, the original spark that caused the cosmos. The cosmos is the consciousness of the Omnisoul, existing before time and space. This may equate to what you earthlings call God."

Ignatius looked at Indigo "I understand what you are saying, but it's a lot to take in. But what about the book? The Charon? What is the event that is actually happening here?" he said.

The priest just smiled sagely without an answer.

But Indigo was keen to keep the questioning going; they needed answers. "Getting back to Calabi-Ya, you said you cannot tell us why the Omnisoul finds him so dangerous. Is that because you don't know, or won't say?"

The old man gave out a big sigh. He groaned a little and rubbed his whiskers with his brown leathery hand. "I… I… I do not know if this is suitable at this time. I do not want to displease the Omnisoul."

A forthright voice came from the doorway. "He is also known

as the Elder God. He is immortal and embodies all that is dark and evil. Some think he is the dark thoughts of the Omnisoul. He has returned because he also seeks the book Turiya."

The old man gave out an angst-filled sigh and, bowing extremely low before Darshan, whispered, "You cannot say that in our presence. It is forbidden… The Omnisoul is infallible."

"Maybe for you, old priest, but for an immortal. I do not agree. I do not fear consequences. What more can the Omnisoul do to the Charon? We are a plaything to carry out orders and cast into Limbo when finished with them. Eventually it must stop. It will stop." Darshan looked angered. She turned and sped off down the corridor.

The old priest shuffled quickly towards the door; his face had flushed. "Enough has been said. Do not ask any more questions, I bid you." He exited and quickly vanished through the labyrinth of corridors and chambers.

Ignatius and Indigo were left once more just looking at each other. Indigo raised an eyebrow. "So what does this Calabi-Ya want with the book?"

"I can only assume to access the consciousness of the Omnisoul and take control of the cosmos," replied Ignatius.

Chapter 12 – The Quest

Together in their embrace, Atman and Tara didn't know how much time had passed. It might have been hours, days or even months. Time no longer related.

Meanwhile, the High Priest of the Ti-Botta opened the huge ornate bronze doors of the vault that now housed the Book of Consciousness, just by waving his hand. The great solid slabs opened smoothly and silently as if they were actually floating. Both Ignatius and Indigo stepped in cautiously. He gestured to Ignatius and Indigo. "Please try."

"I'm not sure I want to know the outcome of this, Ignatius," said Indigo quietly. "Once the book is open, we may have outlived our usefulness."

"Let me open it this time. That's if I can," said Ignatius as he approached the great tome.

The vault glowed green from the great emerald artefact, and as Ignatius stepped towards it his entire expression took on a green grimace. He touched the corner of the gem-like cover and the book hummed and fizzed, a spark of light crackled and encircled his entire arm. Increasing his grip, he attempted to lift the book cover, but it didn't move. The book was locked tightly shut.

"The book knows you have a vested interest. Ignorance is your only chance against this magical tome," said the High Priest.

Indigo took over and as she lifted the cover slightly there was a brilliant flash and all three of them were blinded momentarily. As their eyesight returned it became apparent that although the book was still shut, an apparition had escaped first. A brilliant white light bounced around the chamber looking for an escape and shot off down the corridors. Terrified faces once again became visible. Ignatius tried to open the book again, but the cover would not move.

Suddenly Atman and his consort became aware that they were no longer alone. They felt a strong disturbing presence within the hall. A flash of white-hot light burst through the doors of the Great Hall. The chamber shook. A thundering roar, echoed by a shrill wail, reverberated about the chamber, disturbing the shadows.

From the far end of the Great Hall, a vision formed. A chamber could be seen licked by fiery tongues. In the main, however, the chamber was murky. In the dim gloom, curious pillars soared far above to support the arched ceiling. A lava-like substance flowed down the walls. It was a scene of fractal fire and fury. The floor glistened and dark pools bubbled, giving off a sulphurous gas. In the centre a fire blazed red, beating back the darkness. A hammer struck and a shower of sparks dispersed the gloom. The anvil sang and the smith's muscular body glistened with sweat. His hair and beard were a mass of flames, and drifting around his hammer were fire elementals.

Through the shimmering heat, the two Charon could also see a balding barbaric figure, likely a ghostly apparition, standing behind the blacksmith. Watching, chanting, wailing in harmony with the song of the anvil. With every blow of the hammer, with every fountain of sparks, the figure faded until only the smith and the runesword remained. A sword imbued with the life force of an ancient god.

Scintillating colours swam around the great hall and swirled about the two Charon, orange, gold, amber, scarlet and purple. Crimson tendrils licked at the hall walls, brought to an end when a yellow cloud ascended the chamber as the smith quenched the sword in a pool of brimstone. He embedded the blade in the molten floor, and there it remained until tempered.

Atman spoke, as if quoting from some ancient scripture. "Thus was forged the mighty sword Jeeva, created to fight the Elder God Calabi-Ya, said to be as old as the Omnisoul. But for a different twist of fate, the cosmos might be ruled today by Calabi-Ya and not the Omnisoul. Some legends say that he sprang from the dark thoughts of the Omnisoul, and therefore, the two are but different aspects of the one."

"Whatever the truth, the Elder God was banished into exile aeons ago by the forces of the Omnisoul using the sword Jeeva, and we must find it again to banish him once more."

"But we need to find the whereabouts of the sword," said Tara. The two Charon joined Ignatius and Indigo.

"Let me try again," said Indigo. She stepped forward and holding the edge of the cover, she strained every sinew of her body. Green lightning encircled her, crackling and hissing, shooting up her arms and back down around her waist and one leg. Her chest heaved and her biceps bulged, until the cover opened. She took hold of a silvery page and flipped it over. Before her, a gaseous star cloud formed into individual stars and planets formed from rocky secretion discs. The next page showed a water nymph nursing a knight in armour at the edge of a lake as he choked on his last words, the next showed hideous creatures that looked like mushrooms attacking a black citadel. At the turn of the next page, Indigo gasped as three ghostly figures moved across the page. She arched her back, the emerald light wildly encircling her. A crash of lightning split the chamber and Indigo had to throw herself backwards as the book snapped shut one more time. She landed on her back, boots flailing around in the air.

Indigo's chest rose and fell rapidly as she tried to catch her breath. "I saw something!" she cried. "A tall thin creature… no, a sword, no, a creature… a sentient sword with runes carved all over it. It was in the embrace of a woman, naked… of unearthly beauty."

Indigo's face contorted, her features wrinkled, and she covered her ears. "The noise, the noise, a screech like that of a siren. Three. Three naked women… the creature… then I saw a man, I think, androgynous, tall and slender with three eyes. But one big eye…"

She then collapsed exhausted to the floor. She lay there panting. Ignatius helped her just as Aryas came bursting into the hall, crashing through the two huge rune-carved doors.

"I felt it!" he exclaimed. "What was it?"

"The Watcher," exclaimed Tara.

"Who is the Watcher?" asked Indigo.

"At times, we are helped, at times we are deterred by seven other manifestations, whose nature we are not exactly sure of. Together they are known as the Celestials. The Watcher sometimes gives us instructions in order to help us. The Charon then must execute that will," explained Tara. "What we do know is, the leader of the Celestials is the Master, an all-powerful warlock who can commune directly with the Omnisoul."

Indigo and Ignatius looked at her, puzzled.

"Such is the contradiction of gods. Not all places or knowledge is available to us. Some can die given enough time, some cannot…” Her voice trailed off and she looked at her companions with sadness in her eyes. She questioned Indigo, “And have we obtained any information that is useful, Indigo?”

“I don’t know. I saw a being, tall and thin, maybe with a sentient sword. Or maybe he was the sentient sword, I don’t know. It looked like a steam weapon from my world, features all over it.”

“A runesword!” exclaimed Tara.

“It was in the procession of three beautiful women, their singing almost deafened me.”

The three Charon present all looked at each other knowingly and exclaimed in unison “The Norns! They are in possession of Jeeva!”

“I have seen it in my vision also,” said Atman. “The book has told us so, and the Watcher has led us to the same conclusion. How the Celestials benefit from this, I don’t know.”

“By helping us to exile Calabi-Ya one more time, as they did before,” said Adonai. “They are just trying to protect their own power. We know where the Sword resides. It is deep within the place called Satvaguna. We must make haste before Calabi-Ya also discovers it. We may have within our grasp a means of dissolving this endless cycle.”

“But what about our own mission? We were fortunate to be called using the ancient method and extraordinarily we now have possession that which we have sought for an eternity. What do we do with the book?” said Devi. “For the first time we have the means to end it all.”

“We deal with Calabi-Ya first, it is the only way. But then we must be swift about moving to stop our endless cycle of torment.”

After a little time, the Charon had gathered their battle gear and had given enough reciprocation to keep the Ti-Botta people nourished for a while. Ironically, this was just the sort of thing that led to further worship by the Ti-Botta. It might seem inconceivable for this to be the case, that a god or demon should not know this, but limitations are placed upon all sentient life by the will of the Omnisoul. Yet should the Ti-Botta and other beings stop worshipping them, the Charon would simply cease to exist and be merely a distant memory in the consciousness of the Omnisoul. Or so myth would have it.

Alternatively, if a total lack of the Charon's desire were present, then Limbo could no longer hold the Charon: they have forged their own chains in the furnace of desire and so remain eternal slaves.

The Ti-Botta gathered amidst great pomp and ceremony. The warrior priests adorned in their most colourful finery and playing various instruments lined the streets of the great mythical city. Their music played harmoniously with the sound that constantly emanated from the enormous wind harps that hung over the city, so large they dwarfed the grand city. Several of the Ti-Botta carried the great Book of Consciousness out from its secure hiding place and lay it before Paladin. They backed away, repeatedly bowing, their eyes lowered. He took the book and, binding it with chains as thick as a man's thigh, manoeuvred it onto his back to carry it onto the ship once more.

Devi approached the two Union Jacks. "Come, we are leaving. We now know our quest, and you may still be of use to us should we need use of the Book of Consciousness."

"And after that?" said Ignatius nervously, thinking that the book no longer opened for either him or Indigo.

"We shall see! But surely you are now intrigued, the wonders you have seen, experiencing the true nature of your world and its place in the Hypersphere."

Little by little, Ignatius and Indigo had begun to comprehend just what situation they had got themselves into. With this kind of truth, they knew that their defence of the Empire was trivial by comparison, their steam weapons of no use and most worrying of all, not knowing how they were going to return to earth alive, if at all.

Devi must have guessed what they were thinking.

"Look, you are safe and with the quest we now have there is a chance for the Charon to obtain what they desire the most. So, you will be kept safe and hopefully returned as long as you help us."

She was interrupted by Ignatius who with a grimace said "help? We, mere humans are to help the gods, immortals, or whatever you are. It doesn't figure?"

Devi retorted angrily, her face contorted to such an extent the two Union Jacks thought they were looking into the eyes of a beast from the depths of hell. "Look! We are immortal, demons, and it is usually the case that even those who worship us meet a bloody demise. But you do not understand what we have within our grasp and so you may fulfil a purpose… Maybe you won't. You may die! But right now, you have no choice," and she turned on her heel and walked purposefully from the room.

Chapter 13 – Deliberations

Ignatius and Indigo had no idea and no way of knowing the planes they had crossed, the worlds they had passed through and the very fabric of time they had traversed. They were mere passengers, just cargo with a potential use, currently living in a dream-like experience.

"Well Ignatius, what would happen if we threw ourselves overboard now?" asked Indigo.

"You'll never get back to Oxford" he said drily.

"Where exactly are we going? Where or what is Satvaguna? Is it a city, a planet, another plane?"

"Who knows? But for now, we have no choice," answered Ignatius.

The great ship continued on, gently bobbing on the cosmic wind that carried her, still powered by the burning souls of the deceased. Occasionally, a rogue planet would drift past, having been ejected from its planetary system some aeons ago. At other times, Aryas would have to intervene as a comet or asteroid came too close to the ship, deflecting it with an incantation and a wave of his arms, usually resulting in a sonic boom from pushing the object out of the way with a sound wave.

A little later, the ship passed through an electrical storm, and turquoise lightning cracked and fizzed around the ship.

"Come on," said Ignatius. "I need to fully charge my steam cannon." He pulled a large brass gun from inside his coat.

"Are you mad? What makes you think the Charon are going to let you do that?" asked Indigo with one eyebrow raised.

"If our weapons were of any danger to them, they would have taken them from us by now! But if we are heading for a fight, I think we should be armed."

"In that case, then," Indigo hiked up her skirts and several weapons came clanking out onto the boards of the ship – a derringer, two pistols, a short sword, a steam cannon and the miniature qanun she had stolen earlier. Ignatius could also just see the top of an ornate dagger handle sticking out of the top of her button boots.

"How the hell did that lot fit in there?" Asked Ignatius quizzically with a wry smile.

"A lady never tells," came the retort, "but at least we still have our sense of humour. I can't climb around on this ship or fight with my skirts touching the boards." And with that Indigo undid the buttons on her skirt and removed it along with her petticoat to reveal her long legs and stripy breeches.

"Besides," she said, "my mother used to tell me about the Indian Thuggees, who used to fight in their underthings so they could be silent and stealth like."

"It may be stealthy, but I'm not sure it's very becoming."

She laughed, trying to behave as normally as possible, although this situation was far from normal. "You know how we fight, and we are the best the Union has to offer. Although I'm not sure we will ever return for the rest of our Chapter to see us again…" Her voice trailed off and a little sadness filled her eyes.

As she repacked her weapons, Ignatius asked, "what do you think the qanun is for? I mean, it's a bit small."

"I know. But it must have some significance. The Ti-Botta people seemed to place a lot of emphasis on sound. Those enormous wind harps moaned continually through the day and night."

Indigo examined the qanun. She ran her fingers along several strings. The instrument murmured as if sentient. Gently she plucked a few strings and whilst the melodic soothing sound enveloped them like a velvet glove, the sound waves increased autonomously until the walls began to vibrate and Ignatius could feel his chest begin to throb with pain.

"Stop!" he said urgently.

Indigo held her chest. "Wow! So, it's definitely a weapon, not a musical instrument. We need to take these with us. I have a sense we are going to need them."

"Imagine if we took them back to Oxford. The Administorium would be apoplectic," said Ignatius grinning.

"I don't know why they are so averse to new forms of technology. Imagine if they had succeeded in banning the work of Ada Lovelace and Charles Babbage? They cut off his funding, you know, for his analytical engine and they tried to discredit Ada. Yet they portray themselves as a paragon of virtue. Do you think they could have identified us back at Solomon's house?"

"I don't think so. And even if they did, they can't catch us, at least not at the moment. Imagine if they could somehow follow us. The truth about the cosmos would cause them real consternation. Or of course they could perhaps try and extend the Empire some more."

"I still don't understand why if they are so pro-imperialism, why they try and censor any advancement that seems to come along."

"Ignorance. And fear, I suspect. Remember they were born out of the East India Company and rose to power over a very short time when the Empire was in turmoil and was trying to decide the best course of action when dissolving some of its imperial lands. It was simply cause and effect. At all cost, Britain's technical lead had to be protected particularly when its economic progress was slowing down. For a time, they maintained balance. They infiltrated government and with heavy-handed tactics ruled out any ideas other than their own. It was narrow-minded and ignorant. They represented a new and dangerous form of imperialism. Dangerous because they were so single-minded, so determined that their own policies were the only one's worth deploying they bulldozed their way through all other diplomatic negotiations and outlawed any ideas or anyone who did not agree with them. So when we return...."

"If we return."

"If… So when we return, any technology we can take back with us will give the Union an advantage. On the surface, the Administorium are all bravado, but beneath I think there is much anxiety.

"So do we intend to tell them about God?"

"Hmm. That's tricky. I am assuming the Omnisoul is just another name used in other parts of the cosmos. However, we don't want to just hand ourselves in and be institutionalised as raving mad. Besides, what will the world make of the fact there may be no such thing as free will? The whole of our universe is just the perverse thoughts of a god somewhere. Oh, and he… she… it has written it all down just in case, but no one can access the book successfully to read one hell of a story. I mean we knew the book was important which is why the Union searched for it, but nobody had any idea why. And now besides our own mission, we find ourselves in the middle of some argument between gods, that should be fictitious by the way, and have no idea whether we will die here, wherever here actually is."

They both fell silent for a while. Eventually Indigo spoke, no more than a whisper really. "Then I guess we had better just accept our position. We can't fight it. I only hope that somehow this gets recorded in the annals of the Union."

Ignatius and Indigo had no idea how much time had passed, how much distance they had covered. Did distance even mean anything in the Hypersphere? Somehow without noticing, the ship had entered another plane and they could see land.

The great god ship drifted silently over some unknown city, above the heads of the brigands and pirates that frequented the Inn of the Crossed Swords. None of them noticed the great behemoth above them. Perhaps they could not even see it. Perhaps it was magic. Eventually the great chimneys on board stopped spluttering out the ash of those poor souls that the Charon, the ferryman, had been paid to transport, and the ship gently bumped along until it came to a halt.

The two Union Jacks heard Adonai shout, "Prepare the gangplank."

"We may not have all the answers, but for the time being I think we know where we stand with the Charon," said Indigo, looking at Ignatius with terror in her eyes. "Come on, we'd best go on deck and find out what's happening." The two of them hurried out of the cabin.

Chapter 14 – Battle with the Hell Beings

Dawn paled the eastern sky. The wind was rising as seven terrible beings rode their great black stallions down the gentle slopes away from the great ship. Ignatius and Indigo rode pillion on the back of Devi's and Tara's horses. At times, the Charon looked like terrible reavers, at times hawk-headed, their cloaks torn and tattered and filthy with dried blood. They looked like the hell beings they were. At other times, they looked as Ignatius and Indigo saw them: muscular, proud and regal.

Not one of them looked back as they raced away over the dusty plains where vegetation had ceased to grow. At length they came to green turf and golden meadows where the morning dew glistened in the sunlight.

Birds were singing and wild flowers opened their petals to fill the air with a delicate scent. A few insects wandered carelessly from flower to flower. Darshan gave a faint smile to herself as she rode knee-deep through yellow and pink flowers.

The Charon continued non-stop across the moors and into the foothills, avoiding as many settlements as possible along the way.

They drove deeper into the mountains until they came to a place where the towering black crags opened into a wide valley.

In the distance was a tiny village built in the loop of a meandering river. Streams of prayer flags fluttered noisily in the harsh mountain wind. As the Charon neared, the villagers scattered. Workmen in the fields dropped their tools and ran screaming at their women and children, their loved ones, to take cover. Within seconds, the confused rabble had disappeared and an eerie silence filled the air.

The Charon entered the village and, spurring their horses on, rode straight through at an incredible speed. At that moment, sadness alone filled their hearts.

Through the night and into the next day they continued without rest. Behind them a mass of black rolling clouds began to swirl across the sky like a living entity. The day grew dark and the wind began to howl. Distant thunder rolled; distant lightning flickered, splitting the darkness. Thin rain began to fall.

An ominous storm followed them on their journey.

At length, they came to a vast, sprawling forest. The enormous black trees had gnarled and intertwining roots that rose far above the ground before they joined to form trunks. The rain pattered upon the fallen leaves. There was a discomforting absence of birds and, indeed, all wildlife. However, the place was full of whispers and rustlings and thin tendrils of vapour slithered like wandering ghosts between the branches.

The Charon rode on unhesitant into the dark until they came to the densest part of the black forest. In the shadows of the awful trees, figures moved stealthily. Several hunched figures stared from behind the trees.

Adonai got the feeling he was being watched but couldn't quite make out any figures in the trees. Nevertheless, his senses were on edge. A large hulking shadow slid behind them. Adonai thought he could just make out a huge, bristled arm with an enormous clunking fist at the end of it.

Without warning, sharp, pointed teeth flashed in the dim moonlight close to Adonai's face. But he was too quick and agilely moved to one side enough to avoid the great weight of the hulking beast that threw itself at him. With a rush of feet through the dead leaves, the dark figures closed in on the Charon. The first went down beneath Adonai's falling sword. Blood and entrails spilled over his hand, and something screamed as he ripped murderously upwards.

The nether-beings did not falter, though. On they came, howling and gibbering, long yellowing fangs flashing in the dark. To Ignatius, the beasts looked like some kind of missing link, huge brutish ape-like men with arms that trailed on the floor and cloven hooves that gave firm footing in the soft earth and dead leaf mounds. Their eyes, yellowed and bloodshot, were wild with a savage rage and sunk deeply beneath a bony brow that jutted out from their forehead. Thick, well-developed neck muscles betrayed no existence of any real neck to speak of.

An axe swung blindly in the dark. It whistled passed Devi's face, and a sword flashed. Indigo held her head low behind Devi and stabbed with her short sword at any beast that came near enough for close combat. Devi felt her blade sink deep through hairy skin and bone, and blood spattered her leather corset and chest. Teeth flashed close to her neck, and she could feel a beast's breath upon her face. A hairy knuckled fist smashed into the side of her skull, and she just managed to pull out of the way to safety as Tara brought her blade down next to her face, cleaving a hell-being through the skull and part way down its torso. The scene was rapidly turning into gore as the Charon let loose their fury and beast after beast of the horde fell, creating a carpet of slick crimson under foot. Ignatius had his steam cannon at the ready, and as one hell being lunged towards him, he let loose a shot that tore clean through the beast's chest. It fell in a crumpled heap beneath Tara's horse. Atman screamed a terrifying battle cry and whirled his blade high above his head, and several beasts fell from the trees above. A huge amorphous mound began to rise from the ground, like a beast coming up from hell. As his ancient armour came into view, Paladin rose from a pile of corpses, blood running off his bronze armour in rivulets and his eyes wild with blood lust, having single-handedly killed a great throng of the beasts.

Ignatius had let loose his steam cannon with bolt after bolt of hot shot bursting from the multi-barrelled shaft. Ape-like hell creatures yelped and fell. A scream from behind him alerted him to the plight of Indigo. Dismounted and stood atop a pile of three dead creatures, she was being overwhelmed by another three or four from behind, clawing at her hair and corset. She felt sharp talons ripping through the silk of her corset and tearing at her soft skin. She twisted and lunged forward as the blade of a primitive sword whistled passed her head, just glancing off her shoulder. A cannon shot burst through the skull of the beast closest to her head and blood spattered her face. She heard it fall to the ground with a thud. Grasping a pistol from each side of her corset she gave the last beast both barrels, shot after shot after shot, until it fell onto the pile of death at her feet. As she looked around, she saw Adonai cleave the skull of another and another, and the last wheeled to Tara's sword as she severed through shoulder, breast bone and spine. Standing there spattered with blood and entrails, one of her boots had fallen down and settled around her ankle.

A faint light gleamed momentarily through the shifting clouds to reveal the Charon, blood-spattered and grinning, their eyes full of glee.

All was still again. Misshapen corpses lay in abundance. The dark woods were still and silent once more. These were just beasts of the forest who had chanced an unplanned attack on intruders in their land. Without delay, the Charon travelled on further until the forest started to thin out.

Out of the dimness ahead, a dark featureless blur began to take form. In a clearing at the very heart of the forest stood a citadel. It was a tremendous edifice. This is what the beasts had been trying to defend. Its walls were high and of thick granite. A dense field of towers, grouped so as to shadow one another, topped the walls. The alignment was oddly awry.

"We are here. Satvaguna," said Adonai.

Chapter 15 – The Sword

Beyond the great portal lay an empty hall, the far wall of which appeared at first to be hidden by a grey mist. As the Charon entered further, their weapons ready, it became apparent that there was no far wall. The hall opened into a weird landscape, the colours of which had been bleached.

These were the astral planes – worlds that coexisted, orbited and linked with the universe, entwining it with the Hypersphere.

Here, Prince Aryas felt at ease. The dream-like quality of these worlds gave him much the same pleasure as his drug-induced sleep.

The landscape constantly shifted, making pale shadows flicker. A waterfall cascaded down rocks that hovered in the air, its source invisible.

The Charon took hold of their weapons anxiously. Ignatius held his steam cannon, and Indigo had drawn her short sword. Before them appeared a woman. She was tall and clad in a fine white lace gown, as fair as her skin. A leather corset of powder blue pulled tightly about her slim waist and a jewel encrusted girdle hung low on her hips, from which hung narrow strips of blue silk.

Golden curls surrounded her soft face. Her lips were full and vivid, her cheekbones finely sculpted. The woman took a deep breath and smiled faintly. She had been expecting them. In a soft voice, she spoke. "Welcome. I am Skel. My sisters and I have waited a long time for the coming of this hour. Please feel at ease, your weapons are of no use here, for we co-exist on different planes. Come. Verani awaits us." She led the Charon further into an exotic garden.

She beckoned with her slender fingers for them to follow her. As she walked, she appeared to glide. The curtain of water parted, and she disappeared behind it.

The Charon looked at each other. No one spoke. They had reached their destination. Yet here, oddly, they felt at peace. One by one, led by Adonai, they entered through the waterfall. On the other side, Skel was waiting with her sister. Verani was dressed in black lace, so fine Adonai could see her curvaceous form in every detail through it. She had raven curls cascading down her back. They both had an unearthly beauty about them.

Sweet music filled the vast, circular chamber in which they stood, the upper reaches of which were lost in the darkness. The walls were decorated with hangings of many-coloured silks, embroidered carpets and tapestries. The floor beneath them seemed non-existent, as if they stood in a great void, no earth, no sea, no sky, no air. At its centre, was a large four-poster bed draped in ermine, with a canopy of white silk. A single shaft of moonlight shone down to illuminate the bed. On the bed lay a young woman. She wore a gown of the finest pink lace.

"This is Uror," said Skel. Uror's hair was scarlet, and her limbs were like rose-tinted ivory. Her face was fair, and her soft red lips were slightly parted as she breathed. She was asleep.

In her arms, she clutched a heavy and mighty broadsword, with curious designs upon its wide blade. But it was no ordinary broadsword. Along its length were deeply carved curious runes, in which sometimes it looked as though faces could be seen, as if figures or creatures were trapped within the blade.

Weird and wonderful runes surrounded the bed, beneath the traveller's feet, seemingly painted on nothing, as the floor still could not be seen. The other two women began to dance, trance-like, around the bed. Their skin was as pale as the dawn and as they danced their lace swept through the air, revealing their naked bodies beneath. The two dancers began to sing. At first they sang softly, then more loudly, until their song became a shrill wail. During the singing, Skel began an incantation and arm movements as if conjuring. Ignatius and Indigo nervously held their weapons ready. Darshan, although concerned, leaned in towards them. "Your weapons are of no use in here. Neither are ours." She looked back intently at Skel.

Bright turquoise fire began to glow before them. Within the fire, faint figures could just be seen. Ignatius could see chained, writhing, prisoners enduring what looked like some form of hell. Gradually, the vision faded and as Skel returned to singing, Verani started an incantation and a vision appeared buried deep within blue-green fire. Faint figures could just be seen slumped, broken, weeping, before disappearing again. The singing continued until the bed began to glow and then was consumed by fire. Deep within the flames, Atman thought he saw the faint figure of a blacksmith striking his anvil in rhythm with the singing.

It was difficult to discern the woman on the bed as she sat up slowly. It was even harder to distinguish the outline of a gigantic bald warrior standing beside her, his muscular frame emphasised by the turquoise fire. They seemed to be talking silently. The sword was gone. Atman turned to Tara. "I know, that's the same warrior and blacksmith."

There was a gust of wind through the chamber. The fire flickered madly and then was gone. The music and singing stopped. The woman on the bed fell back, asleep once more. A mighty sword clattered on to the invisible floor.

Nobody moved, unsure of what to do. Uror began to come out of her sleep. As she sat up on the bed again, her red locks fell about her face and shoulders. She looked around, then straight at Adonai and spoke. "The once mighty and proud god Jeeva has committed himself to the forge. He has travelled the cosmos since the first aeon and observed all he wants to see. His sacrifice is your freedom. The power for creating your future is contained in the present moment."

Adonai leapt forward and seized the handle of the sword with all his might, expecting to meet a resistance of sorts. But it lifted easily. He was so quick no one had time to move. He swung the great sword in a huge arc. Ignatius and Indigo jumped backwards to be clear of the blade. Skel was still standing there seemingly unalarmed. The sword went straight through her as if she were a ghost. A great shockwave ran through the void, its occupants became warped and before his eye, Adonai saw images flash. He watched the tip of the sword and its leading-edge slice through a weird rock formation that disappeared as quickly as it had appeared, and then on through the arm of a small boy, wide eyed and terrified; on through mid-air, through the body of a horse. A new landscape cracked, a tree fell, a star fell, he saw humans on earth pointing, amazed at the appearance of a new supernova, until at last all was still.

Adonai stood wide eyed and confused, the screaming that emanated from the sword still ringing in his ears. As he had swung the blade, the sword had hummed as if alive and upon use had begun to scream, the sound waves penetrating other planes, destroying whatever the sword and the sound came into contact with.

Aryas stepped forward, taking the sword from Adonai's now limp grip. He held it out in both arms. He could feel the sentient blade hum and purr.

"Our hearts deepest desire," whispered Adonai. Then in a more awake and deeper voice, he said, "I think that was a Hyperquake, probably still travelling to the outer regions. Time collapsed. Who knows what damage we have caused and who we may have alerted?"

"You must make haste," said Skel.

"The Omnisoul shall know we have it," said Aryas.

"And Calabi-Ya," added Devi.

The Charon exited the chamber, Ignatius and Indigo following close behind. As they headed for the great portal, the three sisters gave them no attention, all congregating on the bed caressing each other and singing in hushed tones. This part of their role in the story of the cosmos, the here and now, was complete. Whether this was written at the beginning of time by the Omnisoul or whether the sisters possess the ability to twist and mould fate is unknown. But as the Charon swiftly left with their prize, they did not hear Skel's whisper: "We are what we think, all that arises within our thoughts and peace comes from within, do not seek it without. Be warned you cannot win this quest alone. There are others from whom you will need help."

Chapter 16 – Calabi-Ya

Out of the blackness, a shape shifted; a dark space, a dark malevolent energy began to grow. The fabric of space began to vibrate until it began to tear, a gaping abyss opened up before the ship Taraka. The distant galaxies formed what looked to be teeth within an angry twisted mouth of oncoming doom and despair.

The ship was buffeted by an oncoming searing cosmic wind. The hot stream of cosmic particles streamed past the bow of the ship, threatening to ignite it. A black shadow engulfed the ship, wrapping its tentacles around the hull and tugging at its unholy boards, attempting to rip them apart. As it continued through the aether, it was buffeted by the wind and its passengers wobbled upon unsteady legs.

"He is here!" exclaimed Adonai. "He has found us."

A young Harlequin appeared in the shadows, unseen on the deck of the ship, and quickly and stealthily made his way over to Indigo and put his arm around her waist and pulled her close to him, surprising her. Despite this, her lightening responses allowed her to thrust a derringer into his ribs. "Unhand me. I would normally say sir, but clearly you are not one!"

Darshan quickly made her way over to Indigo as Harlequin released her, flapping a handkerchief about in exaggeration, placing it to his nose.

"Alas, I wish you no ill, child," he said in a regal voice, although Indigo could clearly detect sinister undertones.

"What do you hope to achieve, Calabi-Ya?" asked Darshan in a controlled fashion, all the time wanting to attack him.

"Now that's a name I haven't heard for some time. Aeons, in fact." He walked the deck with the graceful moves of a ballet dancer. He was never still. His skin seemed to glow and shift, almost as if it was a thin pale disguise. "I believe you have something I require." He laughed. "But first, hospitality. What kind of greeting is this? I mean, I'm almost your uncle. Are we not family?" He continued his strutting, waving his handkerchief.

"Uncle?" whispered Indigo to Ignatius. "The brother to the Omnisoul?"

"Is that what you think?" laughed Adonai striding to confront Calabi-Ya. "You are nothing more than the dark thoughts, the dark perversions of the Omnisoul. Just idle ideas made manifest. Ideas that should never have been initiated. Proof that the Omnisoul is not infallible."

The two lords sized each other up. "No matter," said Calabi-Ya. "But I refuse to be an embarrassment anymore. The Shadow Writings that rule my existence may well be the dark thoughts of the Omnisoul, but, like you, I did not ask to be created. It would seem that my vision is much greater than that of the Charon. Now you have in your possession something I want. No. Not want. Shall be taking with me when I leave. Where is Turiya, the Book of Consciousness, and Jeeva the runesword?"

Adonai ignored the reference to the sword. "And what would

you do with such a book? What plans do you have?"

"With the book, I shall be able to rule the cosmos and take my rightful place in the Hypersphere. So hand it over. You know what happened last time we met. If it's any consolation, I shall never forgive myself for taking your eye. Careless of me, really." Calabi-Ya's face twisted into a terrible, sinister grin.

"You shall never have it," snarled Adonai. "Return to your eternal void, Calabi-Ya, and continue the text in your own book."

Adonai curtly drew his sword to swing at Calabi-Ya. Moving like quicksilver, Harlequin ran around the deck of the ship, impossible to catch or even to see at times. Just a chequered blur and then he was gone. Just silence as the ship continued ploughing its way through the cosmos. The Charon looked warily around them.

The dark velvet of night was suddenly illuminated by the glow of a large yellow orb that appeared in front of them. It was motionless in the inky blackness. The aether around them began to grow warmer. Ignatius expected the orb to grow larger, though he didn't know why. It was closer yet as the great ship Taraka moved through the silent stillness and the orb didn't move.

A faint rasping sound could be heard, and suddenly the yellow orb vanished as a shiny grey membrane moved sideways across it followed by the foulest stench of sulphur. Ignatius's blood ran cold. He looked at Indigo. Both Union Jacks drew a weapon and were ready to move if needed.

The calm was split by a deafening roar as a gigantic jagged jaw lurched forward, dripping sulphuric venom onto the deck, burning holes and giving off poisonous gas. Ignatius and Indigo choked, grabbing their mouths and trying not to breathe. Calabi-Ya had transformed into his dragon form.

Paladin came to help Adonai, attacking the dragon with his

battle scythe, his heavy bronze armour taking the full brunt of the beast's fiery breath. Ignatius was amazed it didn't melt. Perhaps it was protected by some sort of mystical enchantment.

The dragon drew back his long neck and prepared to return for another fiery breath. Sulphur spluttered out on the deck. His huge wings almost wrapped the entire ship whilst his tail came smashing into the bow, knocking Atman and Tara off their feet.

Tara went into a rage, recovering herself and unleashing her sword. Blood lust filled her head, and her eyes began to burn scarlet with hell fire. Her blonde locks looked like white fire trailing behind her head, forming a halo as her face twisted with gnashing teeth. She brought her long sword behind her head and with all her might hacked at the dragon's tail. Again! Again! The long silver blade swirled above her head as Tara came forcefully in towards the dragon's softer underbelly, slicing at the beast's iron scales. Calabi-Ya was nimble, and with great crashing wings encircled the ship, twisting around it like a corkscrew, looking for his next move.

A huge taloned claw came crashing upon the deck. Ignatius and Indigo hurled themselves backwards, landing hard upon the deck. Both of them could feel the heat, their faces growing uncomfortably warm as liquid fire flooded around the deck and headed for their feet. They knew it was pointless. They would be no help against a god beast. "I don't think our weapons will be of any use here," said Ignatius. The two of them retreated towards the stern of the ship.

As they scrambled out of the way to safety, Devi and Atman joined the fray, attacking another area of the dragon's underbelly, his wing beating them off. Devi stabbed at the membrane-like web between the creature's wing bones and took a hold. Sulphurous blood began to seep out. She hung on tightly as the wing beat rapidly, trying to shake her off. Atman's sword whooshed past her head, and he felt it slice scales and bone. A gigantic long snout came driving in to towards him. It cracked his ribs and followed that with sulphuric fire that spread out across the deck all around him.

"I shall have what I came for," snarled Calabi-Ya. "I have been exiled for too long in the cold darkness of the Ghost Worlds. With direction read from Turiya and with Jeeva I shall tear a new doorway, a permanent opening in the fabric of spacetime, and flood the cosmos with my retinue of dark spawn. I shall make my kingdom. The cosmos shall pay, darkness will flood the aether, crossing all planes of existence and the realms of the mind shall burn and those that survive shall worship me. I am due."

Adonai tensed his muscles, causing them to look even more at odds with his beautiful but contorted face. "Then here it is, Calabi-Ya," he said as he uncovered Jeeva, which had been under his cloak. The runesword began to hum and throb lightly in Adonai's hand. The carvings up and down the blade began to sing and glow with an unholy light. The being who had given his life for its creation summoned his entire strength, making the sword hum and spark in anticipation of tasting death. Of tasting scaly skin, bone and sulphurous blood.

Scaled wings engulfed the entire ship, pulling it closer. As if pulling it in for the kill. Bright golden eyes deep set within the creature's long angular skull came closer and menacingly towards Adonai. Adonai could see his own reflection in the narrow slits of the irises. Tendrils of smoke came from the dragon's cavernous nostrils and the last few drops of venom hit the deck in front of Adonai, burning holes where they fell.

Aryas was sat in shadow, cross-legged as usual, chanting though he made barely any sound. Mystical symbols of turquoise fire floated in the aether above his head. The dragon growled a whisper. "I shall not leave without them, Adonai. There is room in my court for the Charon if you assist me. The Omnisoul has reigned too long. The darkest thoughts denied by the Omnisoul should be given a chance to prosper. What say you?"

Adonai held fast with the rest of the Charon behind him. "I beheld another beast coming up out of the earth; and he had two horns like a lamb, and he spake as a dragon. I say never. Your time here shall be but a fleeting moment. You need to return to the Ghost Worlds where you belong."

Collectively and without warning, the noise began to increase significantly. The great runeblade whirled above Adonai's head, the sentient blade singing, sound waves radiating out from Adonai. Aryas, in a trance-like state, began to sing in harmony with the blade. Increasing in pitch, Tara joined them, ringing a singing bowl she took from beneath her cloak. As the pitch increased to inaudibility, Devi and Atman stabbed at the beast's underbelly with their swords. Paladin put his battle scythe to his lips. He filled his lungs to capacity and blew the devil's own tritone.

Ignatius and Indigo felt the bass-like vibrations hit their chests. They contorted in pain and curled up into a foetal position. Darshan headed over to them and engulfed them as best she could to protect them from the soundwaves. "Cover your ears." In such close proximity, Ignatius couldn't help but notice how battle-scared Darshan's body was. Fine lines criss-crossed her body, healed remnants of a life spent at war.

The sound increased until without warning a sonic blast was unleashed and hit Calabi-Ya square on. The great dragon staggered back unsteadily, his wings flapping trying to regain control and maintain his grip on the ship. His angular scaled head swayed from side to side at the end of his long leathery neck. The pain in his head was too much to tolerate. He drew his head back and lunged forward, spluttering brimstone across the deck. Like lightning, Aryas his arms in front of him and met the onslaught with a blast of blue fire from his slender fingertips.

As the great bulk of the beast recoiled, Adonia brought down the singing blade. Reaching its full power, the sword gave out a huge blast that sliced the fabric of space. Paladin blew harder, and Aryas seized his chance. Blue fire crackled from his fingers; his eyes looked like they had rolled back into his head, displaying just the whites with no iris. Incantations continually murmured from his thin lips. As bolt after bolt hit Calabi-Ya in the chest, the dragon recoiled further and further, releasing his grip on the ship. Giant wings flapped, creating a wind that almost knocked the Charon off their feet as the beast struggled to retain his position.

Adonai swung Jeeva one more time, and the beast let out a blood-curdling screech. Another sound wave created by the singing blade and Paladin's weapon hit the beast full on. Two yellow orbs illuminated the dark sky around the ship as Calabi-Ya realised this was the final blow. His eyes widened in terror, a grey membrane flicking wildly across the reptilian irises. Talons reached out for one last, futile slash as the dragon went hurtling back to the worlds between worlds, the Ghost Realm.

Darshan released Ignatius and Indigo from her cover. They were covered in sulphurous soot. Coming out from the shadows, they were just in time to see the jet-black rip in time and space heal itself.

The warriors were all exhausted. Adonai collapsed onto his knees and Devi came into view to help revive him. "Calabi-Ya has gone," she said. "At least that threat has gone. But the Omnisoul will now know what is happening, so we must make haste. We don't have time for rest. We have the sword and the Book of Consciousness and must make our way to the Temple of the Dawn."

Chapter 17 – The Temple of the Dawn

The ship found itself at the edge of a great sea of asteroids, stretching as far as the eye could see. Some were mere fragments of rock; others were almost planet sized, with small rocks in orbit around them. It was impossible to determine a safe passage through them. Ignatius noticed that the great stacks no longer belched the ash of dead souls gathered by the Charon. Everything was still as the ship hung in the aether. Great sails billowed out to catch unseen solar winds that had travelled far from their star systems. The ship continued at a slower pace, avoiding the asteroids as best she could. A small rock floated past Ignatius, who lurched slightly to the left to avoid it. A dangerous place to be, he thought. But then this entire journey had been dangerous and bizarre. He had witnessed the birth and death of whole worlds, travelled through alien landscapes and at one point been revered as a god by some savages on a planet left far behind.

The asteroid field became thicker and thicker until it was obvious that the ship could travel no further without being put at risk. Silently, Adonai turned from his place at the bow, a place he had not left since banishing Calabi-Ya to the Ghost Worlds. Ignatius thought this had been days before. But then, what was time but an illusion, relevant only to the planet you find yourself standing on at the time? In the aether, time was not.

Ignatius saw Adonai's contorted face. His right eye was hidden beneath his bejewelled eye patch, and Ignatius saw him raise his left eyebrow as if in question. From the centre of the top deck, Aryas stepped forward.

He carried a round flask of green liquid in his hand from which coiled a silver flexible pipe terminating in an ornate gold pipe. Aryas held the pipe between his slim, feminine lips. Liquid bubbled and hissed as he smoked it. It was certainly like no other pipe Ignatius had seen in the hubbly bubbly bars and hidden opium dens of Oxford.

In an exaggerated theatrical style, Aryas bowed before Adonai and stepped towards the bow of the ship. It was if the great green flask had erupted to engulf him in an emerald cloud of vapour. Ignatius could just hear a mumble of unrecognisable words as Aryas began an incantation.

Aryas became aware that Tara had taken a place next to him, the two of them sitting in the lotus position chanting and inhaling the emerald tendrils that twisted and squirmed around their bodies as if they were alive.

The darker side of Indigo looked on, mesmerised, wondering what kind of psychedelic drugs they used. On essential occasions, she had taken psychedelics with Ignatius, but only when they believed it necessary to successfully carry out the work of the Union. She had never experienced anything like this. At the bow of the ship, the green vapours had begun to swirl to form a chaotic cloud-like disc that began to morph into a tunnel of living green mass, cutting through time and space as if it no longer existed. A faint tune of low notes could be heard emanating from the ship, creating a soundscape in front of them, bending time and space.

"A safe portal to travel in!" exclaimed Indigo to Ignatius.

The ship entered the emerald haze and drifted steadily along the tubular worm hole. A sweet aroma, almost sickly, filled the senses and Ignatius and Indigo could feel a warm glow filling their entire beings, something akin to having a drink of brandy in copious quantities, but without the alcoholic affect.

With Taraka travelling safely, Ignatius noticed that all the Charon were now gathered together for the first time on the bridge. Even Adonai who had not spoken or left the bow of the ship since their defeat of Calabi-Ya. At one stage, as the ship crossed another plane, Ignatius and Indigo caught a brief startling sight of the Charon in another form. Seven dark and twisted hawk-like hell-beings, something akin to pterodactyls, appeared, partially bathed in blood, with gore dripping from their beaks. Their great long talons had ripped deep grooves into the ships planking. The creature they believed to be Atman looked over at them, his yellow bird-like eyes smouldering with the fires of hell and death emanating from his murderous beak, from which hung, huge clots of congealed blood. One clot dripped onto the ship's deck where it smouldered and hissed like acid. Indigo felt her bowels weaken and her knees quiver. These truly were hell-beings. In the blink of an eye, the hideous sight disappeared, and the now familiar Charon stood before them, Atman grinning a peculiar and sinister grin.

Indigo had turned pale, and Ignatius had to appear brave. He held her close to him, not really knowing what to say or do. This had probably been the greatest adventure any Union Jack had found themselves in. He began to wonder: What would happen when they reached the Temple of the Dawn?

Indigo whispered to him, "I'm pretty sure we are expendable."

"We don't know that," he replied. "But we could examine the book, if we knew where it was stowed. That may help us find a solution to our predicament."

"Or it will tell us our fate! Not sure I want that," said Indigo.

The Charon beckoned them over. "Come," said Darshan. She seemed to be the only one who could put them at ease.

"We are nearly at the Temple of the Dawn—" She got no further before Ignatius interrupted her.

"What is the Temple of the Dawn?"

"It is the centre of the cosmos, but you will know soon enough. But for now, the Charon are concerned for your safety. You need to stay close to us. It is important for you to know that you are precious to us and we will keep you safe. This quest is ours and could be the quest to end all the quests of the Charon. However, I should warn you, your world may not exist by the time this journey is over."

Ignatius staggered somewhat. "What do you mean? Where will we go?"

Darshan gave a small sigh, as if she didn't really want to get into this conversation. It was easy, Ignatius thought, to forget at times that these were super-beings. Gods, in fact.

"That I cannot fully explain, for we don't exactly know the consequences of our quest yet."

"Will the Book of Consciousness not tell you?" interrupted Indigo. "Can we not look it up for you?"

Darshan paused for some time before answering." Not even the book may help us for what is to come. We don't really know. The thought that the Charon may be successful has not ever been contemplated by the Omnisoul, and for that reason I can say no more. The Charon have been set for eternity to carry out the will of the Omnisoul, but we have found a way to—"

She was abruptly interrupted by Adonai. "Enough! We must talk no more of this, in order to keep the quest secure. The Omnisoul is everywhere."

Ignatius was perplexed – these gods were the will of the great god of the Hypersphere, yet they could keep their thoughts secret from him! Aryas smiled at him as if he had read his mind. "You will never understand," he said and turned away towards the bow of the ship, chuckling. "We are nearly there," he announced.

As his words faded, the organic-looking wormhole through which they travelled fanned out and came to an end in what appeared to be a burst of cosmic lightning energy, momentarily blinding Ignatius and Indigo and lighting up the immediate region. A region of space that appeared desolate, empty.

Everything was still. Everything was black. Nothing moved. A small planet appeared some distance away. It was perfectly still, motionless. It did not rotate and appeared to be supported by threads like a spider's web. These were the very threads that linked time and space together. Ignatius thought it was like looking at a three-dimensional simulation of a planet and the surrounding aether, produced by an analytical engine.

"Behold, Omphalos, the Temple of the Dawn!" exclaimed Aryas.

"This is the navel of the Hypersphere, so called because it was the first creation in the cosmos, at the dawn of time. It has drifted in the great expansion and ever since been lost to most beings," said Darshan. "The Hypershere is forever expanding and contracting. I doubt even the Omnisoul even knows where it is now. But it is the centre of all the Hypersphere and for that reason it does not rotate. Exactly where the centre is now is anybody's guess. The Hypersphere is not necessarily a sphere, but aeons of time have allowed us to track it down and find it. Ironic, that our repeated release to do the bidding of the Omnisoul has provided us with enough time to seek it out. We journey there for our quest to end all quests for the Charon."

"And what is the significance of the Temple" asked Ignatius, intrigued.

"It contains the Well at the Centre of Time. The weak spot of the cosmos. Time doesn't really exist there. Legend has it that the Well is the Omnisoul's first thought, the spark of consciousness and therefore the spark that brought about the cosmos. It is the direct link between the Hypersphere and the Omnisoul. The Temple of the Dawn was erected by the Elder God Calabi-Ya over the Well to help find it as it drifts through the cosmos. But I'm sure Calabi-Ya had his own ulterior motive for wanting to keep the place marked. It is a vast complex, the portal to which is reached by ascending an infinite number of steps. To a mere mortal, this would be enough to deter them. A lifespan could pass, and a mortal would still not have reached the doorway. A soul-destroying path to tread."

"As time went by and the Hypersphere expanded and folded upon itself as conscious thought became ever more complex, the Temple of the Dawn entered and passed through the Outer Regions and into the Ghost Planes. These Ghost planes are populated by the oldest planets and star systems that have expanded outwards. Some may even have escaped the Hypershere's shell. They now shadow the known worlds, orbiting them, their planes sometimes crossing. It is here that we have banished Calabi-Ya once more. He had been trapped on the Ghost Worlds before. Until recently, sorcerers had prevented his re-entry and return."

"Will we encounter him again?" asked Indigo, looking

concerned. She thought that dragons were far too treacherous and should be confined to children's stories and legends.

"No, we are quite safe. It will take Calabi-Ya a long time to determine where in the Ghost Worlds he is and on what plane," smiled Darshan.

As they approached the Temple, it looked like a great dark edifice, a black shape upon the cosmic horizon with very few details visible. As the ship got nearer, some detail became evident upon the inky black shape. It looked as if it was made from huge rectangular blocks jammed together at different angles, with one or more enormous round portals covered by a vibrating membrane or a mesh of some description; perhaps a net to capture approaching ships.

As they got closer still, Aryas waved his hand and with a great scream hundreds of drone-like objects were released from the ship, flying around it and producing a protective impenetrable wall of sound – a shield of vibrating aether. They all waited for an attack, but none came. Except for the screaming drones, everything else was quiet, everything else was still. Gradually, the ship moved closer, tentatively navigating its way to avoid the infinite steps ahead of them. As the ship continued, a great staircase came into view. Ignatius and Indigo looked on in awe. The ship sailed on. And on. And on. The steps really were never-ending. Time seemed to slow down, and Ignatius was beginning to think that time had stopped, for this part of the journey seemed to take the longest. It seemed to go on forever. He leaned over the side of the ship to view the steps as they passed beneath the hull, dwarfing even the great cathedral like ship. Eventually, the ship came to rest, presumably at the top of the steps.

Chapter 18 – The Guardian

The object was obscene. It was difficult to identify what it was, god or goddess. This thing was black: deepest, never-ending black. It seemed to absorb the light around it. All colour, forms and objects disappeared into it. And yet, even though the blackness gave no light, it was visible enough that its skin was alive and crawled with life. Life that, momentarily flashed and then faded, hidden from view once more. A seething mass of parasitic life, contact with which would result in pestilence and death. They fed on open wounds upon the skin and the rotting corpses around its feet. This thing, the Guardian of the Well, gradually took the form of something resembling a woman.

An angry face looked down, with three burning yellow eyes and an array of crooked, yellow teeth. A fearsome face. Her tongue protruded from her mouth. It lashed about on occasions and lapped up some of the parasitic life that crawled across her hideous form. Her hair was a living mass of matted hair, with creatures and demons woven into its strands. An entire retinue of flesh-eaters.

Her left breast beat to the destructive rhythm of the cosmos. This was death and destruction, pain and sorrow, fury and bloodlust

– the Dark Secret of the cosmos. The rest of the scene around her was blood-red.

She looked down, her three big yellow eyes blinking with disbelief, and she laughed mockingly at the Charon. The foul stench of hell breath wafted over them, and Indigo felt ill. Ignatius supported her by the arm whilst trying not to collapse himself. He could feel his heart pounding, but somehow regained his strength. He had no option. This was perhaps the most awesome sight he had ever seen. Before too long, Indigo regained her composure and stood fast again, tensing every muscle of her athletic warrior's body.

This was another of the seven Celestials, the only female mystic amongst the wizards who had been transformed to a god-like status after they had defeated the Elder God. She had taken it upon herself to remain with the Temple of the Dawn, to always be at the navel of the cosmos, where their transformation had taken place. It had been so long since she had seen any visitors that boredom and great solitude had set in. Becoming lazy and ill-focused, she had become the form that lay there now. So much time had elapsed that no attack was ever expected, which is why nobody saw the Charon arrive.

In her four arms, she carried a twenty-sided die, a flute, a sitar and a great curved sword that was either rusty or covered in dried blood or both. The sitar was macabre, created from bleached bones. The kaddu, its resonating chamber, appeared to be made from a pelvis and the dandi, its neck, had the curve of a spinal column.

The Guardian blinked some more and tried to focus, still trying to understand what was happening.

"No being dares enter the realm of the Guardian!" she roared. "This cannot be. Who are you? You will find no peace here. This is not a travellers' rest. You must continue on your way or regret it forever." She laughed a ghoulish hellish gurgle.

Surrounding her was a retinue of what looked like an order of militant priestesses. A radical sisterhood who were mostly naked.

"Skin Scribes!" said Aryas. "Their sole purpose is to help protect critical sites around the cosmos, and with a fanatical fervour."

The throng was a countless number of near-naked women whose only dress consisted of strips of cloth fanatically scrawled over with prayers, sermons, incantations, and words of sanctity as a sacred barrier, acting as a psychic barrier against all foes. Some wore sacred relics and symbols of faith or carried ornate icons and consecrated scrolls. Overall, there was a malevolent darkness surrounding them. At various times throughout time, this ugly manifestation was called Legion, for their number was many.

Some carried sacred books open at certain incantations and texts, thrusting them forward at any creature before them, as if to ward them off. They even had sacred runes and texts tattooed upon their bodies - an arm, a leg, a breast, a back. Some were completely naked; their only clothing were the tattoos that covered them from head to toe. Apart from this, their only other visible weapon was their sheer numbers, enough to drag down any offending foe.

But this absence of weapons would soon reveal itself as false. These women were psychers, who with their singing could get into the strongest of minds and attack the subconscious, the most nether regions of the soul and drown a man in his own inner sea of cosmic speculation, his own dark thoughts driving him mad.

One fanatic stood taller than the rest. She was lithe with sinuous limbs, long thighs and arms with a narrow waist nipped just beneath her full breasts. At first glance she appeared to be wearing some sort of close-fitting battle dress. But no, she was almost entirely covered in intricate tattoos incorporating runic texts that started at her heart and spiralled around and outwards from her breasts and down onto her abdomen. Even her legs looked like she wore thigh-high boots of complicated knotwork and sacred runes. Upon closer inspection, Ignatius could see that it was evident her body was also battle scarred. She was a veteran of many hard-won battles defending her faith, defending the Well at the Centre of Time. In her left hand, she bore a huge banner. She was the standard bearer and Herald of the Guardian.

The banner was made of what looked like human skin and painted upon it were the symbols of her legion. At the centre was a stylised image of the Well at the Centre of Time. This was Mahkali, leader of the Skin Scribes.

Adonai was not his usual forthright self. Instead, he was intent on making himself somewhat invisible, standing in the shadows, his head bowed low.

The Guardian became distracted, and she giggled and moving her many chins scooped up some minion-like creatures and devoured them. Then snapping back to the present, she looked down. "Are you still here?" she boomed.

At this point, Adonai revealed himself from the shadows, his shock of orange hair falling about his shoulders as he dramatically shook his mane and staring up at the ugly beast with utter disgust, spoke.

"You are a disgrace to your host, oh Guardian. A being who has destroyed itself with sheer laziness and slothful ways. The aeons have taken their toll upon you."

"Who dares—" but the Guardian didn't finish her sentence as Adonai shook his mane once more and his jewelled eyepatch glinted in the dimness. A look of horror came over the Guardian's face as recognition gradually took a hold in her mind.

"The Charon!" she screamed attempting to stand up as creatures fell off her foul bulk. Suddenly the Skin Scribes became aware and began to mobilise and close in on the Charon and the two Union Jacks.

Chapter 19 – The Abyss of the Mind

This would not be just a battle using weapons, this would be a transcendental challenge, for this would ultimately be a battle within the labyrinth of the mind on the Astral Planes and could render a mere mortal insensible. This would be a battle that could destroy the very souls of Ignatius and Indigo. The battle would manipulate the very nature of being, to influence life itself, to twist and reduce any creature's very being, but not, as the Charon desired, destroy them. The Charon knew even an immortal could mentally drown if they lost focus during a battle such as this. Perhaps an appealing option for members of the Charon. This was where the Inner World of any living being met with the Outer World of Reality. The battle had the potential to destroy the soul's entanglement with the unbounded ocean of reality and, therefore, lead to an eternity in the Ghost Worlds, the domain where the subconscious can run amok.

Paladin stepped forward and although his armour gave him power enough to make him the most powerful of all the Charon, it was his hell-forged battle bladed instrument that would be the most useful.

When and how the mind begins to leave its trace upon the fabric of the cosmos is one of the great unknown mysteries. The whole cosmos is influenced by every thought, word and action of every individual life form within it. The unconscious mind is the untapped omnipresent power of the cosmos, with the power to forever change the cosmic tide. Struggles upon the battlefield pale into insignificance when a being has cause to contend with inward enemies of the mind.

In his mind's eye, Aryas stood alone, in the dark void. This ocean of dark matter is what binds life to the cosmos, to the First Cause, the Omnisoul. This cold dark matter swirled and gathered mass, accumulating molecules within the mind warped space somewhere within the nether regions of the Hypersphere until there, before him, stood the Guardian. Around her swarmed the horde of Skin Scribes, screaming a siren song that could pierce a being's soul.

As Aryas sat motionless in his usual cross-legged pose, Paladin fell in beside him, blowing on his bladed weapon. Blast after blast hit the horde of Scribes, felling them, but they regained their feet and continued to close in on the Charon. In the mind of Aryas, the great black mass of the Guardian engulfed him. Devi, Atman and Darshan waded into the great multitude flailing their swords to the audible crunch of bone. Adonai was seen amid the thousand-strong legion, atop a pile of dead bodies, his ears bleeding with the shrill singing. This was the physical aspect of the battle, but the real battle was going on in the mind of Aryas.

Aryas sat alone with the Guardian, locked within the energy well that had enveloped them. The deep energy well warped space and time, threatening partial entropy. The darkness was fast turning into a brilliant white energy field, only to be replaced again by deep velvet blackness. His face had become distorted, and sweat appeared on his furrowed brow. In the depths of his subconscious, Tara joined him. She was actually sat cross-legged beside him. Butterflies flew around the inside of her skull until they morphed into long-fanged leathery creatures that gnawed at her brain. She cried out. Without opening his eyes, Aryas gripped her arm, his knuckles turning white. His ears were bleeding and tears rolled down his cheeks from his now pain-wracked eyes. Despite her trance, Tara felt the pain of his grip on her arm. In the mind plane, they had combined force and were now engaged in full combat in their dream quest. The Guardian was difficult to pinpoint in the darkness, her great black amorphous bulk fading in and out of their minds. Aryas murmured an incantation, and the void became bright turquoise. A bright yellow star passed by. It rose and set in quick succession and continued to do so over and over, but the intensity had revealed the Guardian. She could hide no longer. Faint whispers of worlds came and went.

Ignatius held his head. His eyes were wild and bulging as he turned to Indigo, "there is someone in my head and it's not me!" His muscular frame staggered around violently. He tried to pull out his steam cannon, not really knowing who he would aim at.

Indigo had terror painted upon her face as she flung her arms around Ignatius, pulling him closer. She cupped his ears with her hands and looked him square in the face, screaming "Leave him! Leave him!" and holding her forehead to his, she pulled the miniature qanun from her garments and released Ignatius. She began to play, her fingers moving in a furious blur across the strings. Ignatius felt the vibrations hit his chest, and the melody travel through his body. He felt at one with the vibration of the aether around him, and the pain in his head began to subside. He could feel his body grow weightless and as his body floated, presumably somewhere on the

Astral Planes, he could look down on himself, his wracked body struggling to handle the situation at play in his head. As the siren song subsided, his out-of-body experience ended and his astral self re-joined his body.

Just then, a smartly dressed white haired man with a furrowed brow and long nose appeared before them. His features were very sharp and his skin was pale, his eyebrows white. He was wearing a bowler hat, a black jacket and tie, sporting pin-striped trousers, carrying a brief case with the letters MR embossed on the top by the locks. As he opened his eyes, for they were shut, a look of sheer horror and panic moved across his pale face.

"This isn't Cambridge! Or the Royal Society! Where am I?" A look of complete puzzlement on his wrinkled face. "My God!" he exclaimed as he looked around. "The Anthropic Group and Theosophical Societies will never believe me. They'll think I'm mad!"

And with that, he promptly vanished again. Although this was the world of emptiness, it was an aspect of consciousness that was a further state of dreamtime where a state of mind can be used to cut through the illusion of the everyday world and achieve insight on the Astral Planes. In times gone by, these planes were virtually empty whenever Aryas would traverse them, save for a few shamans or holy men. But today, surprises were appearing at random. Aryas saw a holy man sitting cross-legged, deep in meditation, seeking the Truth. He was dressed in orange robes and a long string of beads. He had a long white beard and long white hair. His face resembled old brown leather and upon his forehead he wore a painted red symbol that travelled down towards the bridge of his nose. He sat perfectly still and smiled knowingly at Aryas until he vanished again.

A long-haired young man passed by, dressed like a Bohemian

traveller. Aryas thought the youth's dilated eyes were going to pop out of their sockets as he stared at him. "Far out, man!" he cried. "This is awesome!" Clearly this was a novice experiencing some hallucinatory drug-induced state. "Hey man, it's the Gypsy King" he cried, obviously mistaking Aryas for some idol or another.

But even Aryas was a little confused when he thought that out of the corner of his eye he saw a white rabbit run past carrying a silver pocket watch. The cosmic lake of the inner mind was a strange place.

His lapse in concentration cost him though, as the Guardian was suddenly right in his face. He could see the veins in her yellow eyes throbbing and he felt tentacles start to wrap around his body, squeezing him, crushing his bones.

In the cosmos of reality, Aryas and Tara were unaware of the huge number of Skin Scribes that were surrounding them. The rest of the Charon battled on, their weapons slicing through flesh and bone, and yet the multitude kept coming. Rivers of blood flowed around their feet.

Unusual for the two Union Jacks, Ignatius and Indigo were hesitant to get involved. They seemed unsure of their capabilities in a cosmic world such as this and whether these Skin Scribes were human or god-like.

Ignatius and Indigo looked at Aryas and Tara, still sat together, seemingly motionless. Aryas's clothes had begun to darken with sweat. Tara had begun to show signs of some discomfort and to claw at her leather battle gear, but between the two of them they chanted in unison a spell that the Guardian could not make out. Aryas still had a grip on Tara's arm, but this was no chance action. The two of them had conjoined their minds, melded their power, and suddenly they both multiplied upon the Astral Plane in which they battled. Multiple copies surrounded the Guardian, the turquoise light growing more intense.

Linking hands, they formed a circle around her, and their chant began to grow louder and louder. The Guardian clumsily swung her four arms around, but it had no effect. Two of her arms urgently started to play the sitar she was holding. She put the flute she carried to her fat blue lips and began to play an eerie, high-pitched tune. Both tunes were designed to counteract the sound waves coming from the Charon. The void began to distort. It ebbed and flowed, over and over, building to a crescendo. The Guardian's yellow eyes began to bulge in disbelief and terror. She lashed out with her sword, missing the two Charon. The Charon could vaguely hear the song of the Skin Scribes somewhere in the background, but undeterred, they continued. The Astral Planes began to weaken, and at times the two of them faded in and out of the void. Aryas's free hand reached into his coat and pulled out a glass vial, sipping from it between lines of his chant until it was empty. His body grew in strength, and his insides warmed due to the drug he had just taken. His belief grew. He was stronger than ever. The multiple copies of Aryas multiplied again, increasing the width of the circle around the Guardian.

His grip on Tara increased. Blood trickled from beneath his fingers and with one final chant, the sound waves hit the Guardian square on, rippling through her own melodies, cancelling out frequencies and washing over the Guardian like an ocean. It knocked her to the ground. Her mountain of flesh rippled with the sound waves until it became too much and her body ripped apart, exploding and hurling flesh and gore everywhere.

Aryas and Tara collapsed in a heap, exhausted from their mind games with the Guardian. Aryas groaned, his breathing shallow. He tentatively opened his eyes, wiping the stinging sweat away from them so that his blurry vision could reveal the still bulk of the Guardian lying where she had originally sat, a blot on the cosmos, a stain on the spacetime fabric of the Hypersphere. She no longer stood in their way to reach the Well at the Centre of Time. But as they looked around, they could see the rest of the skirmish still unfolding before them.

Chapter 20 – Carnage

As the throng of marauding Skin Scribes continued their attack, Devi swiftly retaliated with her broadsword, cleanly cleaving the skull of the first marauder. As she pulled her sword clear, the horde pressed on, singing their shrill siren song. She felt bone crunch as she thrust her sword into the rib cage of another and wrenched upwards to splice her heart and exit at the shoulder. There was a gurgling sound and abrupt halt to the singing as warm blood spattered across Devi's face.

The crimson liquid ran down her pale features and trickled onto her lips. She experienced the hot metallic taste and blood lust took over. She swung and thrust her sword like a true demon. Blood, bone and entrails flew through the air. The atmosphere was hot and sticky with the gore, the floor slippery.

Scores of hands clawed and pawed at Devi's body from all directions, pulling her down. The Skin Scribes were overwhelming, tearing her flesh and her clothes. Singing and chanting overwhelmed her, and blood-spattered Devi could hardly breathe. Blood continued to rain down as she continued swinging her broadsword. Her raven hair was drenched crimson, her flesh sore from the sheer numbers attacking her. Gradually she disappeared into the sea of flesh. Another throng of near naked and gore-stained bodies piling up to form a mound, a great bulk of tattooed flesh and carnage. Eventually from the centre of the heap, Devi rose as she killed the last few remaining Skin Scribes attacking her. She climbed out onto the peak of the mound of grotesque death and destruction for which she had been responsible – a sea of entangled bodies, a scene of absolute horror. Rising, she stood aloft, triumphant in her battle. One boot was missing, one breast exposed. Blood dripped from her hair onto her rapidly heaving bosom and ran down her thighs. In her left hand, she clutched the tattooed head of a Skin Scribe.

The scene sent a shiver down the spines of the two Union Jacks.

Tara looked across to Adonai and Darshan, who were surrounded by corpses. Darshan's blood-soaked blouson now matched her red leather boots.

Adonai let out a battle cry as he swung his great wide battle blade two-handed over his head in an arc. It was a perfect slice through the skull of a Skin Scribe. Warm blood and brains splattered onto his hands. He expertly swung his blade to the right, cutting another down as she ran towards him, splitting her soft tattooed belly and spilling her entrails onto the floor.

Ignatius and Indigo found themselves surrounded as the Skin Scribes continued to close in on them despite their best efforts. Several fierce-looking and fanatical Skin Scribes dashed directly towards them. Ignatius had already taken position. His stance was rigid, his body locked, one foot in front of the other as he raised his arm, ready to take careful aim. His chest was beating; he could hear the sound of his own heart in his ears as he waited to fire. Indigo aimed her steam cannon and drew her short sword. There was a bright yellow and red flash followed by a hiss of steam swirling up into the air, and the lead Skin Scribe stopped in disbelief as the shot tore a large hole in her chest. The eruption of blood sprayed the others around her and as she fell, her naked twisted body was trampled by those who followed. Wailing and singing, they came at the two Union Jacks like a swarm of insects.

"They are not gods!" Ignatius shouted to Indigo. "They die!"

Short sword at the ready and a steam cannon in the other hand, Indigo threw herself among them, drowning in their siren song. Her cut and thrust felled two more , momentarily clearing a path through the marauders. She could feel the clawing of hands trying to pull down. Limbs began to encircle her. Too many limbs. With swift movements of her blade, a Skin Scribe lost her hand, another some fingers. A flash of blade and Indigo felled two more, one holding her belly, the other holding her throat, her siren song now no more than a gasp. Ignatius coldly and calmly uleashed blast after blast, steam hissing and surrounding him like a mystical cloud. Another fell as shot from Ignatius's steam cannon whistled past Indigo's ear. This was more like the battles they were used to, against foes who could be hurt, injured, killed. Although they were supernatural, their bodies were like those of humans. The Union were trained for this kind of fighting, and Ignatius and Indigo were prime among their peers. Even so, there were too many, and Indigo disappeared beneath the horde of tattooed flesh and prayer-scribed banners. The last thing Ignatius saw of her was the terror in her eyes and the miniature qanun she slipped out of her garments. Ignatius did the same. Furious fingers plucked at strings, and the vibrations from the two Union Jacks intersected with each other. The horde of Skin Scribes began to stagger, holding their ears, their singing falling to little more than a whisper. Indigo crawled from beneath the pile of naked bodies and jewel-encrusted icons, her corset blood-spattered and torn, and re-joined Ignatius. Together, they readied for the next wave of warriors.

"So traditional weapons work," she said panting for breath. "But sound technology is better."

A wild-eyed Skin Scribe came running at him. She modestly wore a thin girdle of dirty white fabric on her tattooed body, which had prayers or spells written all over it. As she neared, Ignatius pulled the trigger. Steam hissed again and when it cleared, he could see a hole right through the once-muscular abdomen of the Skin Scribe. Silently, in disbelief, the Skin Scribe moved her bald tattooed head down to gaze at the hole in her midriff before falling to the ground dead.

Encouraged, the two of them let loose volley after volley of shot, temporarily keeping the horde at bay. The two Union Jacks were successful at holding the mass back, but one tall and heavily tattooed Skin Scribe got close and grabbed Indigo around the throat. Indigo twisted quickly and struck her attacker with the pommel of her short sword. Blood flecked her corset, and before she could be attacked again, Indigo swung her blade and caught the Skin Scribe on the arm, splitting an ornate tattoo. As the Scribe yelped, Indigo wasted no time. Lining her blade up with a tattoo on the woman's left breast, she thrust, plunging her blade through ribs, hearing them crack before piercing her opponent's heart.

Paladin strode purposefully forward. "Enough of this," he exclaimed. He expertly arced his weapon like a scythe, slicing through three Skin Scribes before him. But instead of changing the arc to swing back, he brought the handle of the great blade up to his lips, pausing momentarily. The rest of the Charon saw this and, thrusting their enemies aside, quickly covered their ears. Darshan urgently bellowed at Ignatius and Indigo to do the same.

With that, Paladin filled his lungs to bursting, his chest expanding against his ancient armour, and blew, his fingers dancing along the keys in a rapid dance of gauntleted fingertips. He started to grow in stature, his human-like form beginning to change. He turned black and looked like he was made of rock, like basalt, which started to crack and reveal fire and brimstone within. The cosmos surrounding them trembled and shook, the shock wave echoing out, the intensity of it bringing a bloody rain of burst flesh pouring down as the remaining Skin Scribes exploded with the force. A seething landscape awash with gore and bodily parts lay before Paladin, such was the force of the resonance he set up with his musical weapon. He returned to his normal self, blood running down him, painting the front of his bronze armour crimson.

Vomit lay before the two humans, their stomachs churning in abject horror at the ghoulish nightmare before them. Their eyes bulged, thankful their ears were still intact, although ringing a little. Ignatius knew that sometimes, great armies going into battle would play loud music to put fear into their enemies and cause psychological terror, but he had never seen anything like this, nor would he want to again. Paladin looked around, his grisly white teeth grinning through the blood staining his face.

"I only hope I do not need that much strength for any fight later."

As they all looked around, the Temple of the Dawn was awash with gore, its great black blocks and vibrating membranes were stained crimson, its black marble steps flowing with the blood of the Skin Scribes. In the middle lay the behemoth of the Guardian. All was still, all was silent.

Chapter 21 – The Well at the Centre of Time

Deep within the vast complex of the Temple of the Dawn lay Yukteswar, the Well at the Centre of Time. The task now was to locate it amongst the piles of the dead.

The Well was the remnant of the First-Born Star, the very first thought of the Omnisoul. Its remnants now formed a neutron star. The fabric of space around it curved so severely it spiralled and formed a wormhole, a well so deep that nothing could escape it. Over billions of years, the First-Born Star had exhausted its nuclear fuel, the remaining dense matter ripping through the cosmos to an unknown destination in Hyperspace. This was the weakest point in the fabric of the cosmos and evidence of the fragile nature of the balance of all matter and beings in the Hypersphere.

The floor was slippery under foot due to the carnage. Sticky blood flowed everywhere. As they all approached the centre of the huge Temple of the Dawn, the two Union Jacks could see what must be the Well at the Centre of Time. As Indigo looked on, she thought the well looked like a huge singing bowl, but slightly moist and glistening. It was like a living organ, an orifice deeply connected to the living cosmos.

At the heart of the Well burned a ball of gas, hanging in the dark, bottomless void. The fire warmed the Temple. The Charon could feel it warming their faces. Each of them could vaguely remember experiencing something similar in the distant past, but they knew not when. Unknown to them, this was their very birthplace.

The seven Charon stood looking at the Well. Devi looked over at Adonai and gave him a faint smile. Atman shot Tara a glance. For aeons, the Charon had longed for this moment. The moment in which they might all find rest, their hearts' deepest desire. To put an end to their immortal existence of bloodshed, war, and horror.

Ignatius looked nervously at Indigo. They were both thinking the same thing: This was it, their time was up, and they never really knew how they got mixed up in this. They had been seeking out a book of knowledge to protect the Empire, sure, but had had no idea their actions would lead to this. They'd had no idea that Skye would harm their Chapter of the Union Jacks and destroy their mission.

"I still don't understand how we came to be here. What did Skye do to lead to all of this?" said Ignatius.

"She was descended from Calabi-Ya, a daughter of the Elder God," said Aryas as he stepped close to them. "The same way you are descended from Adonai," he whispered to Ignatius.

The Union Jack looked at him, his face pale, contorted with horror. The birthmark on his hand was burning again. A great yawning chasm opened in the pit of his stomach. He thought his legs would buckle. Sweat covered his brow and his head swirled. His eyes were full of anger and hate. His twisted face looked towards Indigo. She recoiled from him.

"But how?" He felt his legs weaken beneath him.

"At times a god, a demon, a ghost, an immortal, may find the

Omnisoul preoccupied, and when crossing the planes on his travels, break the boredom with some illicit enjoyment. I think your world calls him Spring-Heeled Jack!" Aryas gave a dark, sinister grin, a full row of teeth displayed mockingly. A red haze crossed Ignatius's eyes, and for a moment Aryas resembled a hawk-headed man with tattered clothing. The clothing of a reaver. Blood dripped from the end of his yellowed beak and he carried a scythe, encrusted with congealed blood. Then the scene before him became normal once more. He shot a look at Indigo to see if she had seen it too. She was holding herself, wide eyes fixed on Ignatius.

"No! I don't believe you" said Ignatius as he rubbed his chin in frustration. "I am not descended from that!" he spat giving Adonai a look of complete disgust, the image of a hawk-headed man burning in his mind's eye, "from him!"

He reached out to hold Indigo's hands and she pulled further away from him. Surrounded by the co-agent he loved, and the gods he had travelled with, Ignatius had never felt so alone. Screaming tore through his head, a silent scream, madness, insanity threatening to set in.

Aryas reached out his long-fingered bone white hand with its ruffled cuff and gripped the top of his head. "Calm yourself! Humans are such fragile beings. Think about it. When you were standing outside the old man's house, you felt something, right? Some sense of what was occurring. There was a connection to the events unfolding in that very bleak vault."

Ignatius looked once more at Indigo. She looked crushed, tears rolled down her soft and blood-spattered cheeks. "You betrayed me! Betrayed the Union!"

"Indigo, I swear. I didn't know. I have only ever worked for the Empire." He looked at Adonai once more. He was standing with his arms folded across his huge muscular chest, a proud and defiant look upon his beautiful face. The birthmark on Ignatius's hand burned even more. He looked down at the source of his pain to see that the birthmark had changed colour. It was redder than before. He thought about it. He had felt it: he'd known some event, something unplanned was occurring in the house.

"Does that make me a demi-god?" asked Ignatius. He looked up at Aryas through his pale fingers.

Aryas released his grip. "No, that's only in stories," Aryas grinned. "You are only human, but there is and always will be a connection between you and Adonai. It's the result of cosmic entanglement and aeons of planning by Adonai."

Darshan came over and spoke in her usual soft tones. "You have an important part to play in realising our fate. To bring about the end of the Charon."

"But how?" said Ignatius, looking more puzzled than ever.

"I'm not sure, but all shall be revealed shortly, no doubt."

Indigo, sat looking on, still holding herself. A thousand thoughts raced through her mind. She dried her eyes and composed herself once the worst of her thoughts had abated. She patted down her garments and adjusted her weapons, professionalism restored once more. She was a Union Jack, an agent of the Empire. She approached Ignatius slowly and reaching out took him in her soft warm arms. Holding him tightly she whispered, "Sorcery, it's all sorcery. Ignatius, forgive me." She shot a glance at each of the Charon looking on. Returning her gaze to Ignatius she said "I'm sorry, it was such a shock and insensitive of me. How you must be feeling… I love you, my friend, and we must get through this. We can do this." She looked at him square on and gave a weak smile of encouragement.

Suddenly, a great thud shook Ignatius and Indigo.

The Great Book of Consciousness was chained to Paladin's back. Each chain link was as thick as a man's thigh. The great warrior removed the book from his back and began to unshackle the tome, which started to glow even more emerald and to hum quietly. He placed it at the feet of Ignatius and Indigo. They both looked at him inquisitively.

"I guess this our moment," said Indigo. She turned towards the Charon, knowing her best defence here was her confidence.

"Open it!" demanded Adonai, looking at Indigo, his tone harsher than usual.

Indigo knelt, the skin on the underside of her chin began to glow green as it reflected the light from the great book. As she touched it, the book began to hum and throb. Emerald lightning cracked and snapped about her arm. Her body buzzed with the power the book was now exuding. Gripping the edge of the cover, she tentatively tried to lift it as green fire danced around her body. The cover did indeed lift and the book opened. Although unlikely, it appeared to them all that Indigo hadn't gained any vested interest in the book. Surprised, she looked at Adonai and then at Ignatius, who feared for her safety. If this was all that was required, then Indigo might have outlived her usefulness. Images flashed across the first page of the book as if floating around in mist. Indigo touched the page, and it purred like a cat being stroked. The images rippled and changed. Again. And again. And again.

"Where do you think I should start?" she asked as she turned the pages back and forth. Each time she did so, the scenes and words that had once appeared on the page vanished and were replaced by another. The lives of ordinary people were playing out before her: children at play, warriors dying on the battlefield, a planet flying by, gaseous nebulae, some kind of unfamiliar and alien creature foraging for food, an asteroid crashing into a rocky planet. She thought she saw Devi, then Tara, and then they were gone. Nothing in the book seemed stable. This really was a book of random thoughts and ideas.

"I can show you" said Adonai, "but I shall need Ignatius to help."

Ignatius looked surprised but was intrigued. "That mark on your hand," said Adonai.

Ignatius looked at his hand. "It's just a birthmark."

"Is it? Come here." Adonai took Ignatius's right arm and momentarily placed his hand over the jewelled eyepatch. "Not everything that has come to pass has been by chance. We have been looking for the Book of Consciousness for so long in order to end our infinite limbo, our lack of free will. We discovered the book had been placed on your plane, but we didn't know which realm or which time frame. So, whenever I could, I left a safety net. My union with other beings left a part of me spread widely across the cosmos, for I knew that one day I would need my full sight. It was taken from me by Calabi-Ya during a previous battle to prevent me from seeing the pages of the great book. A one-eyed being can never perceive the plan. Although as you already know, there are different rules that apply to all gods, to all beings.

Adonai continued. "The Omnisoul may control the collective consciousness that is the cosmos, but the greatest weakness in the creation is the Norns. They are able to have an influence on events and to some extent create fate. Whilst the Omnisoul has been watching us carefully, the Norns have been able to manipulate the events leading to the here and now. The only side-track has been Calabi-Ya. Nobody expected him to return from the Ghost Worlds. Just unfortunate events. However, we have more pressing matters."

Returning her attention to the book, Indigo turned a page. The same misty silkiness swarmed, and hazy images came and went. She delved deeper into the book and turned more pages.

Adonai looked at Ignatius. "I need my eye," he said, and placed Ignatius's hand over his eyepatch once more. The birthmark looked like a tattooed eye, perfectly matching Adonai's other eye, and the two of them looked on as Indigo continued to turn pages.

Ignatius felt power surge through his body. his chest expanded, and his engineer's waistcoat seemed like it was going to burst at the seams. His consciousness drifted across cosmic planes; a myriad of colours filled his vision. He was with the stars. He was a star, orbiting inside a galaxy. He heard the cosmos breathe and heard the beating of its heart. He was at one with Adonai, at one with the cosmos. It unnerved him, and he hoped for it to end soon. He hated Adonai for creating in him the ability to help the god see.

Tara had started to grow impatient. "How much longer? We need some urgency. This is not the time for family reunions!"

"What can you see?" asked Atman with hope in his eyes.

"Too much!" came the reply. "But I haven't yet found anything pertaining to the Well and our fate.

As all of the Charon were concentrating on the book along with Indigo and Ignatius, none of them saw the tall slender figure floating behind them.

Chapter 22 – The Stalker

A tall slender figure who seemed to be hidden in his own shadow stood watching The Charon. "Your plan will never work, Adonai!" The sharp voice shattered their concentration.

All nine of them spun around, startled at the intrusion, annoyed they had all managed to let their alertness lapse. "The Stalker!" cried Devi.

The figure came forward but still seemed to be shrouded in his own shadow. He must be dressed all in black, thought Ignatius. But he appeared to have no face, no eyes, just a slit of a mouth. He moved silently. "This can only lead to disaster, Adonai. There is no way the Omnisoul will let this happen. I have been sent by the Master to bring you back. Your quest has ended. Calabi-Ya has been banished to the Ghost Worlds once more, and the rip in spacetime has been repaired and reinforced to prevent a repeat of his entry."

Adonai turned away from the book, brushing Ignatius aside. "There is no way we are returning this time. We have come too far, set in motion too many plans, and the Celestials are not going to stop us. You can continue being the Omnisoul's puppets if you wish, but we are done. You and the other sorcerers have risen to your positions by choice. We have not!"

"The Sleeper is on his way to take you back to the Keeper. You will not be able to stop him."

Indigo stepped forward. "And what is to become of us?"

The dark figure quickly snapped back. "You are not my concern. The Charon haven't killed you yet, so that's a bonus, so far." He gave a sinister, hellish grin. "Perhaps it is apt that amongst everything, the Charon want freedom, and yet they have enslaved you and the man." More grinning followed.

A blast exploded to the right of the Stalker, but he didn't even flinch, just glided slightly more to the left. Steam drifted up from Indigo's hand as the steam cannon hissed and reloaded automatically. "Indigo!" screamed Ignatius, "He'll kill you!"

The Stalker tutted "You don't want to test my patience, young girl. The power of the Celestials can crush you to a single atom if we so wish."

"We are dead anyway," she screamed at Ignatius.

Darshan stepped forward and restrained her, removing the steam cannon. Indigo could feel her muscular but slender arms in a vice-like grip around her. "It will have no effect" she said, "the Celestials are in possession of the most powerful magic in the cosmos. It is the Omnisoul's cruel joke. For the moment, you are safe. Let's work with that, shall we?" Indigo fell limp, her shoulders dropping as she gave up all hope.

Paladin took a firm grip of his of his battle blade and shuffled uneasily. He wanted to cleave the Stalker's skull. But, in truth, he had no idea whether that was possible, such was the power bestowed on the Celestials by the Omnisoul.

"I have no intention to fight," said the Stalker. "I am not going to waste any more time here, either. You cannot win. Now I have found you, the Sleeper is on his way. I shall leave it to him. But of course, the Omnisoul by now must be aware of your plans." He flicked his slim hand at the Book of Consciousness, released an insidious laugh and with that he faded back into the shadows and was gone.

Chapter 23 – The End of Time

"We must move quickly," said Adonai and returned his attention to the book.

"I refuse to turn any more pages," announced Indigo. "If I have no future, then neither will you."

"We have no choice," pleaded Ignatius. "We have no way out of this, but at least if the Charon are successful, perhaps we can return home. The Union shall be all the poorer without the knowledge we have gained."

Indigo let out a yelp as Tara pushed her and Ignatius in the back abruptly, herding them back towards the book. No more was said, and all of them set about the task. Page after page was turned. Emerald light illuminated them all. The book purred and pages shifted as the sentient thoughts of the Omnisoul became more apparent, at least to Adonai.

Times past, present and future writhed across the surface of each page. Whole worlds came and went, individual beings lived out their lives for Adonai to see. More worlds were conquered, destroyed and born again. Stars formed from burning gas grew in size and exploded in supernovae. Empires rose, were conquered and fell. Plots were hatched and executed or abandoned. Beings that even Adonai had never seen before crawled across the page and disappeared again. Adonai searched intently for the Charon's destiny, forged and fixed at the time the book was created. "There!" said Adonai abruptly, a frown upon his face. There! There... I have seen enough. The sword. No, the sitar. No... It's gone! It's gone!" he screamed. Such was the fickleness and complexities of the Omnisoul's mind. "We may not see it again, it's impossible to search the entire history of the cosmos from beginning to end, but I believe I know enough."

Indigo tried turning another page. It resisted her touch, and emerald fire sparked around her arm. It snaked its way up her arm and twisted itself around her body. She looked terrified as the sentient fire caressed her and restricted her movement, increasing its grip. Her wild eyes, now burning with green fire, looked for Ignatius in desperation. A loud crack split the aether and blinding green light momentarily stunned them all, including the Charon. Then silence resumed and Indigo fell into a crumpled heap.

Ignatius rushed to her and took her in his arms. He looked at Adonai, who almost had compassion in his voice: "She will be ok, but the book may no longer be of use to us."

Indigo began to stir, opening her eyes. They had returned to normal. "Here, drink this," said Aryas, handing a vial of orange liquid to Ignatius to administer. "It will give her strength."

Moments after drinking the liquid, Indigo was restored.

"The Omnisoul has been wise enough to prevent us from being able to open the book, and now has taken away that freedom from the only person who could, the daughter of Atman," said Adonai. He looked at Indigo. "You are the product of a union under Aryas's spell. An enchantment so powerful he was able to completely mask your identity from the Omnisoul. Due to its nature, it's an enchantment he has only been able to create once."

Indigo wasn't sure whether to be horrified or not. Ignatius saw her shoulders drop. She was exhausted, physically and mentally. Her heart pounded and her lungs filled to bursting, pressing painfully against the whale bones of her corset. They had both been pawns in some game of the gods. Her mother, what had she done? What of her poor father? She needed to know more, but she couldn't think straight, and this was clearly not the time. Reluctantly accepting her situation, but failing to comprehend it, she shot a mean glance at the dandy-looking Aryas, then at Atman, who was his usual calm and quiet self. He turned away, ignoring her gaze. Aryas shrugged and giggled, throwing his arms into the air.

Not wishing to delay any longer for fear the Omnisoul would soon try to stop their plot, Adonai decided he had enough knowledge and sprang into action. The affairs of humans paled into insignificance, but their part in this quest was only just beginning.

Ignatius caught sight of a red blur alongside him. It was the behemoth that was Adonai. The muscles on his back rippled and almost burst from his clothing as he lifted the broad-bladed runesword Jeeva high above his head and rent asunder the ground beneath them, all out of sheer frustration and anger. His face was taut with rage, but hope burned in his eyes.

"This ends now. We will destroy time. Without any time, the Omnisoul cannot exist. We cannot exist. We have the power to do so, provided by the Norns and Jeeva himself. He gave his life for this moment." The sentient runesword sang gently in his hands.

Ignatius became aware that all of the Charon seemed to have a yearning in their eyes, yearning for their life to be as they wanted. Without losing any more time, Adonai headed for the Well. He ran his hand around its rim. Placing the Sword Jeeva almost vertical, he started to run the sword around the rim. The Well began to vibrate and sing. The song rang out across the cosmos, growing loud and ominous. The whole of the cosmos was filled with sound, a roaring unending sound that pierced and penetrated every particle in existence. Adonai removed Jeeva, and the fabric of spacetime continued to vibrate with the sound of the infinite consciousness. A single sweet low note vibrated through Ignatius's whole body.

The battle for the end of time was here. The Charon had fought throughout time and throughout the cosmos, but this was the most important. They had defeated the Guardian, defeated the Skin Scribes, and no other foe stood before them. The sound was all there was. Ignatius and Indigo covered their ears, but it was of no use. The sound penetrated their every being. The vibrations passed through them, causing every atom of their being to match the frequency of the cosmos. Ignatius noticed that gradually the tone was changing. The sound got louder and louder and shock waves began to radiate out from the Well. Was this the screaming in the Omnisoul's head?

Paladin put his battle horn to his lips and blew with all his might. His ribs expanded enough that he could feel them pressing against the inside of his ancient bronze armour once more. The sonic blast travelled towards the Well. Upon reaching the Well, the blast covered it, encircled it, but seemed to dissipate as if it had hit a protective shell. Aryas came to his aid, and as Paladin blew again Aryas muttered an incantation and with both arms outstretched sent a bolt of lightning towards the Well. It travelled alongside the next sonic shockwave and hit at the same time. But the Well still stood.

Adonai plunged the runesword into the depths of the Well. Nothing. No destruction. Jeeva had failed to damage the Well, much less destroy it.

Indigo gripped Ignatius by the arm. "If he destroys time, is that it? Are all our lives lost?"

Ignatius shrugged. "I guess so, but there is nothing we can do. We are mere pawns in all of this. It seems even our lives have not been our own. But at least we can say we fought for the Empire and never wavered. That must count for something, right?" Even Ignatius wasn't convinced by this.

The sweet sound from the Well suddenly turned into a frenzied orchestration of unhinged notes that filled the cosmos. Elsewhere, the whole cosmos vibrated and shook, stars tumbled and exploded, supernovae filled the voids between worlds, nebulae burned, gas discs formed and where worlds were destroyed, new ones were born in the fiery burning aether. Infinity continued, the cosmos endured, the consciousness of the Omnisoul re-formed.

Suddenly and without warning, the Well erupted into an effulgence of light. The space around it warped and twisted. The giant blue-skinned head of a four-faced god emerged from the light. Its faces twisted and contorted, one with anger, another frozen in a twisted grimace, and another in a hideous sinister laugh. Some faces looked like that of a man, others like that of a woman. The many-armed god swung weapons and musical instruments left and right. Other arms carried a crown, an orb and a sceptre. The figure was adorned with skulls, and both snake and animal skins draped across one shoulder. Instead of hair, flames raged from the top of the god's head. Prayer bells rang, and Ignatius and Indigo thought their ears would burst. This was the genderless Omnisoul.

The multiplicity of arms allowed the Omnisoul to perform several tasks at once. Several weapons and musical instrumentals all burst into action. Hands twisted gracefully into different poses as if part of a dance, others played a flute at the lips of one of the faces, others swung a sword, a spear, two others played a lute and the whole symphony of the cosmos went into disarray. The music of the heavens was chaotic and out of balance. The sound from the Well had been absorbed and replaced by the resonance of the Omnisoul. Fire burned in each of The Omnisoul's eyes, and suddenly one great head leered down to gaze upon Ignatius and Indigo. The two humans could see their own reflection in the eyes that gazed upon them, blood-spattered and battle weary.

"Are these Asura? An insult to my creation! They think themselves powerful superhumans, demigods or demons?" boomed a great fiery gruff voice, the stench of foul unholy breath making the two of them feel sick.

"He… she… it thinks we are demigods," whispered Indigo.

"What are you doing in the realms of the gods? To what end are you here?"

Ignatius didn't know what to reply.

"The humans are mine, they are with me," interjected Adonai.

At that, the giant blue figure frowned at Adonai, flames erupting from many heads. A rage set in as one of the faces spotted the Book of Consciousness. A roar boomed out over the music, unbelievable anger took hold and whole galaxies died as a result and the cosmos whimpered in response.

"You will feel my wrath for your insolence!" All chaos erupted, the very ground beneath the two humans twisted and warped, the very fabric of time and space rippled and stirred, the heavens above and below spun, stars tumbled and burned brightly, whole systems died in that instant. The great multifaceted head of the Omnisoul burned and gushed forth towards them. It towered above them and let out an almighty roar once more. Enormous snarling teeth dropped venom in front of the insignificant Union Jacks, and snakes struck forth hissing as if the Omnisoul's hair was made of serpents and fire. Great yellow eyes burned with hellfire. The humans went weak and their legs trembled, nearly buckling beneath them.

Abruptly, as if like a dog, the great head loomed high above, howling, and Paladin could be seen clinging to the pony-tailed flaming hair behind the Omnisoul and landing several blows to the side of one of the great giant's faces. None of the Charon were quite sure what was going on, none had ever dared to directly attack the Omnisoul. But this was different, there was no turning back. The Charon had never come this close to ending their eternal limbo without free will. This was their time. Their destiny.

To the side, Tara and Devi were whirling their weapons in a blur so great that a meditative hum was given off that seemed to calm the spacetime in their immediate vicinity.

The break in intimidation for the two humans gave them the chance to return to the book. Indigo grabbed the emerald cover. "I have no vested interest in my own fate. We die here today, and I have accepted it. So let's try the book one more time."

To her surprise, she lifted the cover and it opened with a crackle of lightning. Images swirled across the pages. She continued turning the pages in desperate hope to find something that might help the Charon. Ignatius tried to join in the fight, but soon realised that blasts from his steam cannon had no effect. The Omnisoul just absorbed them.

Suddenly, Ignatius tugged on the back of Indigo's corset sharply and pulled her backwards onto her back. A bolt of pure energy shattered the ground next to her, missing the pair by inches. Although occupied with battling the Charon, the multifaced Omnisoul was still able to keep the humans in view. A shrill, piercing, high-pitched song knocked the two of them further back with the sheer force of the sound as a female face of the Omnisoul appeared so close the gleam from an ornate gold filigree crown momentarily blinded Indigo. As Indigo reached out trying to find her way, she touched one of the faces of the Omnisoul. Despite the youthful female form the head appeared to have, the skin was like leather, and it burned Indigo's hand. She yelped and withdrew quickly. She held it against the silk of her corset, waiting for the pain to stop.

The Charon battled on, but the Omnisoul was too powerful. This was a fight they couldn't possibly win, but they were desperate not to return once more to their perpetuity. Midbattle, Atman stopped and stared. Blood ran down his face from a head wound. How had it come to this? *If only our injuries could be fatal*, he thought. But he knew in his heavy heart that they were not. The cycle would begin again, and the Charon would do the Omnisoul's bidding over and over for eternity.

With his muscles rippling through his red clothing, Adonai hurled himself between The Union Jacks and the Omnisoul. While Paladin, Darshan and Tara kept the Omnisoul busy, it gave Adonai a break long enough to use the magic eye on Ignatius's hand as Indigo still flicked through the sentient pages. "There!" he murmured so as not to be heard too loudly. "I have the answer, the sitar and the sword."

Chapter 24 – Infinity Shards

The aether throbbed with the sound of battle. Holding his breath, Adonai moved swiftly, abandoning the battle to make his way over to the motionless bulk of the Guardian. The great shape of lifeless darkness was still being poured over by parasites. One of the strange creatures with green skin caught hold of Adonai, and he slapped it aside as if it was an insect. With all his might, he lifted the dead weight of her limbs until he located the sitar she had carried. The sitar was an odd structure that looked like it was made of bleached bone. The resonating gourd, or body of the instrument, looked like a combination of a pelvis and ribs, with the dandi, the neck of the sitar, looking like it was made of a spinal column. Pulling it out from underneath the great dark obscenity, he took the runesword Jeeva and inserted it along the neck of the sitar. This meant that the sentient runeblade, which after all had once been a god, could not only reinforce it but would add to the resonance of the instrument with its own singing when the sitar was played.

As Adonai returned to the battle, Aryas saw him approach. "Samardi, the Cosmic Sitar. You have created Samardi, once played by the Omnisoul at the creation.

Adonai seated himself cross-legged on the floor. The battle around him seemed to pause as all looked to gaze at him. The Charon wondered what he was about to do, not yet understanding the nature of the sitar and the sword. The rest of the Charon surrounded him to form a shield. Ignatius and Indigo took cover and protected their ears. Devi followed them and threw her cloak over them as more protection.

"A magic cloak?" whispered Indigo.

The Omnisoul raged uncontrollably, muscles popped, hair flamed fiercely as if suddenly fed with fuel, serpents hissed, and foam frothed at the mouth of every face.

Adonai plucked at the strings of the Cosmic Sitar; his hands were a whirl. The music rang out across the cosmos and the sound waves penetrated the Well at the Centre of Time. Wave after wave of sound vibrated, passing through the Well, right to its core. The Well sang at the same frequency, multiplying the sound level and intensifying the melody from the Sitar.

As the music grew louder and the sound waves more intense, Adonai stood up and began approaching the Well. The Omnisoul swung wildly, several arms just missing Adonai. The rest of the Charon fought back in defence and parried each blow or near miss. Paladin was instrumental in forcing the Omnisoul to retreat a little.

"How dare you. You are mine! You are my minions, my playthings, this revolt will not be tolerated anymore," boomed the Omnisoul. Even hidden beneath the protective cloak, Ignatius and Indigo could feel the Omnisoul's voice pound against their chests and ears. The ground trembled and they could feel its vibrations. "Traitors, you will have your wish. I am the Omnisoul, your creator, your master. I have no more use for you. Limbo shall swallow you for eternity, damnation shall be your only acquaintance forever."

Even Tara and Atman, who were just in front of Adonai, were struggling with the intensity of sound. But before too long they stood with Adonai at the Well at the Centre of Time and Adonai began to compose a special note, a universal note so deep, so loud, with such frequency that the two Union Jacks thought they would faint. They felt weakened and struggled to stay conscious. They looked on, just peeking through the folds of Devi's cloak in time to see Adonai, a wild look in his eye, plunge the resonator bowl of the Sitar into the Well with all his might. Weakened by the music, the Well was torn asunder by Jeeva. There was a terrific explosion and the sound shot out from the epicentre as a great bow wave that travelled across the whole cosmos. Nothing stood in its wake. The very fabric of time and space cried out. The Omnisoul cried out. The biggest Hyperquake ever emanated out and began shredding all matter and all time. The ripple passed below Ignatius and Indigo, momentarily throwing them into the air. The Charon lost their footing. Lightning cracked and shot out from the Well, and the Temple of the Dawn began to crumble, its great dark pillars collapsing. The noise from the Well sounded like the whole cosmos screaming. Ignatius witnessed whole worlds burning, stars died and exploded into supernovae or just simply dissolved until nothing remained.

Indigo shed a tear, saying quietly to herself, "I wonder if the earth survived?"

Adonai and the other Charon looked on, expecting to see time and space start to dissolve before them. Adonai believed they had successfully slain time, destroyed it, destroyed their reason for being. "Timeslayers," he shouted grinning, looking directly at The Omnisoul with defiance.

As Ignatius and Indigo looked on, having crawled out from

beneath the cloak, they could see the look on the Charon's face change to puzzlement.

There had been destruction on a grand scale, but instead of total destruction, the Well had split into an infinite number of shards, each containing an intact copy of the Well at the Centre of Time. Surrounding each Well were seven terrible beings, war-torn and tired. The Charon were looking on at… the Charon. Each shard of space and time was identical to the next. As the bow wave made its way across the cosmos, every particle it touched split into an infinite number of identical particles, and so identical copies of the cosmos were created, each entwined around the next, an infinite fabric of space and time, multi-dimensionally entangled, and each identical cosmos was a perfect holographic image of the next.

As the futility of it all dawned on each of the faces of the Charon, and the Cosmic Sitar music began to fade as it reached out further into the distant cosmos, the cruel laughter of the Omnisoul, who had now vanished, could be heard echoing all around them. A hideous, mocking laugh that resonated through the cosmos, mocking the Charon's failed triumph and the fact that the Book of Consciousness had now vanished also, the Omnisoul reclaiming it on departure.

Adonai fell to his knees, sweat and anger flowing down his face. And faintly, just audible above the cruel laughter, Ignatius and Indigo thought they heard a super-god crying.

Ignatius looked at Adonai, at the complete disbelief etched on his deathly pale face, his cheek bones looking even more gaunt than usual. Here before Ignatius was a broken god. His one visible eye reflected the immense pain shared by all the Charon and also reflected the cosmic shards that seemed to drift in slow motion away from them, twinkling like jewels in the cosmic sea. The whole of the cosmos had vibrated with such a force that it had fractured from the blow the Charon had inflicted.

"This is not the result the Charon were after," said Ignatius as he stood fast with Indigo. Without realising it, they had both drawn their weapons in anticipation. "Time may be up for us, at least."

They both jumped as a sudden scream ripped through the unnatural stillness. In unison, the Charon screamed.

"It cannot be!" shouted Tara her face so contorted, so pale she looked like a ghost of herself. "We have not succeeded in slaying time. We are not free, eternal damnation continues and now it is multifold!"

The two Union Jacks didn't understand what she meant Until they stared at the shards more intently.

"The whole is present everywhere" whimpered Adonai, broken. "The Omnisoul has created a self-reproducing cosmos. We are everywhere… it is true, we are Legion, for now we truly are many."

"We cannot break the manacles that bind us. Perhaps this has always been so," added Devi.

If they were going to make a move, now was the time thought Ignatius, but his feet felt like lead. He looked at Indigo and he could see she thought the same. If the whole was everywhere, they needed to find their part of it and try and return. But maybe that was an impossible task. Really, they were helpless and stranded, their faces displaying total disbelief. Perhaps this is where they would die. Perhaps an Ignatius and Indigo would live on somewhere else.

"I should have realised. Perhaps there were clues on the Astral Planes?" whimpered Aryas. "The irony. We will always be immortal."

The aether around them shook as somewhere, the Omnisoul sounded Shanka, the great conch shell, to mark a passing. Not of the present, for the present, the past and the future are everywhere at once, but to perhaps mark the end of the current epoch. The battle was over, and the Charon had lost. They also knew that shortly the Sleeper would be on his way to return them to Limbo.

This had been their greatest quest. The Charon were broken. They had saved the Hypersphere from Calabi-Ya, banished him yet again. They had tried to destroy the Well at the Centre of Time, to destroy the very consciousness of the Omnisoul. And failed. Adonai, exhausted, looked over at Ignatius and Indigo.

Ignatius and Indigo looked at each other. They too had sadness in their eyes. This wasn't their quest. Not the one they had set out on. Not the ending they wanted. They had no idea whether they could ever return to Oxford, to England, or to their own time. At that moment both the Charon and the Union Jacks shared the knowledge that it takes colossal strength to grasp a fate.

As the multiple Hyperspheres began to get used to their new form, used to their entanglement, with more reasons for the Charon to be used by the Omnisoul, somewhere, on the many planes of existence, a super-god could still be heard crying softly.

Chapter 25 – The Return

The Union Jacks had no idea how much time had elapsed since their visit to Solomon's house. They knew that time really was an illusion and that events could take place at the same time. It was not necessarily linear. How this would benefit the Union, the Empire, the Empress or the Earth even, they didn't yet know.

As Ignatius and Indigo stood on a fragment of spacetime fabric that had once surrounded the Well at the Centre of Time, they looked at each other with blurred vision. The sky and the very earth about their feet became a mosaic that started to crumble and disappear piece by piece until they were standing in a void. No land lay beneath their feet. As they continued to stare, awestruck and feeling bleary-eyed, an image began to reassemble about them until they were standing on the deck of the great ship, traversing the heavens once more.

"Will we ever get back?" asked Indigo.

"I think there is a more urgent question to be answered first. Will we survive to get home? The Charon have no reason to keep us alive," replied Ignatius. "Either way, the Administorium have no idea what the cosmos is really like. They live in fear, oppressing others because of their technological and scientific advances. Yet none of this is really the threat. It's all the other lifeforms out there, the alien life, the countless gods, the superpowers and the power of sound that they, that we, know nothing about that is the real concern."

However, the two of them thought it was reassuring to know that some of these gods had limitations and it seemed that some of them could even die. They could be governed by rules and laws that either limited or enhanced their powers. Immortality came with its own issues: loneliness, a feeling of repetitiveness, a lack of free-will. They had travelled across the cosmos and travelled to the very heart of it, learning more about the very nature of reality and whilst Ignatius and Indigo felt somewhat enlightened, they felt very much surplus to requirements.

Their thoughts and conversation were halted as they were overshadowed by the crimson giant that was Adonai. "Fear not! You are both safe. It would seem that the Charon must continue, though we do not accept this fate. However, we will return you to Oxford before the Sleeper finds us and returns us back to the Keeper. You have both fought valiantly. Without you, the Charon would not have been able to fulfil this quest. You shall not die today. We may need you again one day, my son and daughter of Atman. No matter how long the Omnisoul keeps us chained with the Keeper, no matter what Limbo or eternal damnation we face, we will never accept our fate and will continue to find ways to change it, to end it."

The two Union Jacks were uneasy at the reminder of their lineages.

"My only advice to you both is don't get addicted to being human. It is only temporary. The Hypersphere, or the Megasphere now, has many secrets, many wonders, some of which you have learned. But there is far more you do not understand. Your body is just a vehicle that you may leave and enter as with any other vehicle."

"Good luck," smiled Darshan with sad eyes. "We have never met such unusual humans before. You have fought bravely and are worthy of your heritage. We will meet again in some future, on some plane."

Ignatius and Indigo felt the great ship Taraka begin to move, the great funnels above them churning out ash once more. Indigo felt a chill down her spine. The Sleeper was probably in pursuit, threatening to return the Charon back to Limbo at any moment. The Union Jacks wondered if their journey would end before the Sleeper carried out his task. Ignatius put his arm around Indigo and together they closed their eyes, hoping for peace, for rest, for a quick return to earth.

They didn't know how much time had passed, but after some well-earned rest, the Union Jacks opened their eyes and winced at the brightness. Sunlight pierced familiar white fluffy clouds.

As they reappeared outside Solomon's house, with no sign of the Charon, wisps of smoke from the walker's blasts still rose and swirled into the morning air, making dreadful patterns like hideous ghosts. They were home in Oxford, though they didn't remember getting here. Perhaps they had been in some magically induced sleep?

Later that day, there were reports that Spring-Heeled Jack had been seen terrorising the citizens of Oxford again, a shadowy blur of red with a blue cloak, before disappearing again.

The Board of Inquiry were meeting in the Administorium to discuss the events of the night. It seemed that there had been no witnesses to the murder of the academic Solomon or the unknown girl who lay beside him, however gruesome her demise. The drones had sighted some potential assailants, maybe as many as nine, but had failed to capture any evidence of who they were. The only result of the inquiry was that a further inquiry was required.

Ignatius and Indigo looked at each other. "Oh!" said Ignatius, "I think we need to get you back to the house before too many people start to fill the streets." Indigo looked puzzled, until it dawned on her that she stood armed to the teeth still in her undergarments.

"Ah! Good idea" she chortled, and the two of them made haste; Ignatius led the way, anxious to get back to his study to research deeper into sound power.

Epilogue

Report Number: 01/1856
Type: Classified
Agent: Isambard Ignatius
Chapter: House of Albion

Before reading this report, I warn you that it will sound incredible, and my soundness of mind will be called into question.

The quest Indigo and I undertook to look for the Book of Consciousness was successful in part. The book was obtained but has since been taken by other forces to a place inaccessible from earth. The Union Jacks are unable to make use of it, but so are the Administorium, and therefore the Empire can rest at ease: It is impossible for the secrets contained therein to be accessed.

The greatest success of this mission has been the advancement in our understanding of cosmology. For thousands of years, mathematicians, astronomers, scientists and academics have been impressed by the order of the stars in the night sky, the clockwork regularity with which they travel. Many have speculated on their nature and what really lies beyond our own cosmic shore, theorising on the nature of reality, and our rulers have long since looked to the heavens to expand the shores of the Empire. I hope this report will form the basis of future expeditions and research into our access to the stars.

Our current understanding of the cosmos has been shaped through esoteric thought and scientific observation. Scientists today do not know how the inflation in the ever-expanding universe began, although it is thought by some scientists that because some mechanism has happened at least once before, then it is quite possible for that same mechanism to begin again. For a long time now, we have thought it's possible for a part of our existing universe to suddenly inflate or bud and grow another universe. It is for this reason that some physicists believe that the universe as we know it may not be alone. Indeed, it may not even be unique. We may inhabit a bubble that is part of a vast array of universes or even parallel worlds that float within the grand cosmic ocean. It is possible that a whole series of planes or higher dimensions may interpenetrate with our own world or universe and with each other to form a complicated structure far more intricate than we can comprehend. It may be that without realising it, we cross these other planes throughout our lives, maybe during that time between wakefulness and sleeping.

I should warn you that with our ever-increasing understanding of the cosmos and all the matter within it, ideas and views that we have always thought to be true may crumble when scrutinised and analysed further. There is evidence to suggest that our world and everything in it may be just ghostly images, projections from another level or plane of reality that is beyond both space and time. At times, it would seem that our esoteric thought may be the foundations of actual science and what we often believe to be a figment of our imagination has turned out to be the truth, contradicting traditional thought.

Scientists within the Union talk of the celestial harmony of the heavens and the music of the spheres. Music is nothing more than a sound wave, a vibration of matter. Matter consists of particles that we now know have a wave nature. Therefore, all living matter is nothing more than vibrations in the cosmic ocean, affected and connected by the vibrating waves of all that surrounds it as they spread out like the waves on a pond.

Some religious thought over thousands of years has believed that the dynamic force of creative energy within the cosmos exists as sound vibrations. Even our minds are affected by these vibrations, for all life forms are linked to this resonating ocean of energy. Many ancient religions have discovered that ultimate reality can be found in the chanting of a mantra, a sacred sound that if executed correctly can vibrate at the same rate as the material around us or the universe, which is in a constant state of vibration. The result of being in harmony with the vibration of the cosmos is that an individual can join with the universe and be a part of the energy field that surrounds and binds all matter; to be a part of the all-containing sacred sound, the cosmic consciousness. All actions and movements are musical, made up of vibrations that reach out and interact with the higher planes. The mystery of the universe lies in sound, sound that can radiate outwards like ripples in a pond when a stone is dropped into it. This is the effect caused by every atom, for every atom is alive; there is no such thing as dead matter. Therefore, every action really does have an opposite and equal reaction, whether it is in our own world, or further afield in another. All life has an effect on the cosmos; all life is inextricably connected. We have witnessed weapons that use sacred sounds to destroy matter and believe the

Union should begin investigating such weapons immediately. I request permission to start such investigations.

Mind or consciousness is not just a product of physical brain activity. The mind lives in matter and the two are inseparable. This means that our bodies are not a separate entity to the universe. We do not inhabit a certain point in space; we are a part of that space, a part of the whole. Most of the particles in the visible universe exhibit a high degree of entanglement. Knowing we are literally stardust as the particles in our bodies were created in a star might mean when a star dies and explodes into a supernova, particles could be separated across the vast ocean of the cosmos, meaning that particles in us may be linked to particles elsewhere in the universe or in another lifeform.

This mission has answered how these particles are created and, therefore, how life is created. We have encountered supernatural forces that have played a key role in the creation of the cosmos along with the significant role the Book of Consciousness played. But this cannot be discussed here as the Empire, indeed the world, is not ready for such knowledge, so I am requesting a meeting with the First Lord of the Union Jacks as my information is above classified.

I. Ignatius
Oxford

Glossary

This tale has grown and developed in my mind and developed on paper over a very, very long time. In creating this story, I have tried to choose names for places and some characters that are significant in some way rather than have names that have been invented. By doing this I hope that the story will carry some meaning as well as a view of how the cosmos may be arranged and the place humans occupy within it. Listed below are some explanations for the names used.

The Administorium. An organisation set up to monitor technological developments within the Empire, with a view to understanding whether they are good for the Empire or will bring about harm in some way. The members of the Administorium then decide to allow development to continue or bring about its demise. No one knows whether they are self-appointed or were instigated by the crown.

Akashic Record. In Vedantic Hinduism, Akasha means the basis and essence of all things in the material world. In the Western mystic-religious philosophy called Theosophy, the word Akasha is used as an adjective, through the use of the term "Akashic records" or "Akashic library," which refers to an etheric compendium of all universal events, thoughts, words, emotions, and intent ever to have occurred in the past, present, or future in terms of all life forms, not just human. It is believed all thoughts, words, and intents generate their own unique "frequency or vibration", which is stored in the Akashic Records on the "mental plane." In Sanskrit, the word Akasha means sky, aether or atmosphere.

Al Kimiya. A variation of the word alchemy. Those trained in the art of Al Kimiya are wizards. Ragnar of Roc was engaged in magic when he blundered and let the great dragon Calabi-Ya return from the Ghost Worlds.

Angevins. The Angevins refers to three separate royal houses in the 12th and early 13th centuries; its monarchs were Henry II, Richard I and John. The Angevin blood line from which Skye is descended stemmed from Richard I, the Lionheart, from the House of Plantagenet, born in 1157, and Lord of Anjou. Subjects of the Plantagenet's claimed that Satan himself was the ultimate dynastic founder. In this case, Satan has been identified as the Elder God Calabi-Ya.

Aornos. Aornos is Greek and is interpreted as a place without "without birds," giving rise to the legend that no bird could fly across it and live because of its poisonous sulphurous vapours. Surrounded by dense forests in ancient times, it was represented by the poet Virgil as the entrance to Hades. Skye uses this term as a reference to the language of the birds – a perfect divine language used by mystics to obtain and understand great wisdom. Seeing that Solomon was struggling in his understanding of the problem before him, Skye uses its term as a joke. The book he reads obviously is not in the language of the birds.

Aryas's Chant. The words Aryas chants when trying to open the Book of Consciousness, "Shaktipat, Nephesh Chiah. Sahaja. Ohm maneee arrsharoo. Ong namo gurdev namo," have some meaning. In Hinduism, Shaktipat means the transmission of spiritual energy upon one person by another. Nephesh is a Hebrew word meaning sentience – life or soul. Chiah is fictitious but can refer to being creative. Sahaja is Sanskrit and means born together at the same time. Ohm refers to soul or the self within. Manee is a play on the word mani, and means jewel, as in the chant "ohm mani padme hum" meaning praise to the jewel in the lotus. Arrsharoo is fictitious and a play on the Hindu name Sharu, meaning gift of God. Ong namo gurdev namo is a corruption of Ong namo guru dev namo, meaning I bow to all that is.

So as Aryas sits upon the emerald book he is really chanting something like "Transfer this energy, this soul, this creative jewel, this gift of the Omnisoul, for I bow to all that is in the cosmos."

Asura. When Ignatius and Indigo are at the Well at the Centre of Time, they are addressed by the Omnisoul, who asks if they are Asura. In Buddhism, Asura is the lowest rank of deity or demigod.

Calabi-Ya. The Elder God, the great dragon. Almost as old as the Omnisoul. It is thought he might even be created from the dark thoughts of The Omnisoul. The name derives from Calabi-Yau, a particular type of algebraic manifold used in theoretical physics, particularly in superstring theory. This manifold is itself named after Calabi, who theorised its existence, and Yau, who proved Calabi's conjecture. Every point in our universe's three-dimensional space may contain six additional compact dimensions that we cannot see. Physicists refer to this realm as a Calabi-Yau manifold. Therefore, it suggests that although he is banished to the Ghost worlds, Calabi-Ya may be all around us, everywhere in the cosmos but without any means of getting in. The Elder God is the first manifestation of darkness within the Hypersphere; the first division within the consciousness of the Omnisoul to form dark matter and energy. This cold dark matter swirled and gathered mass, accumulating molecules within the mind warped space somewhere within the Nether Regions of the Hypersphere until it began to conquer and feed upon the light. The dark energy of the Elder God lies entangled within the extra unseen curled-up dimensions of the Hypersphere, the Ghost Worlds, scattered so to become less of a threat. From time to time, this energy gathers and dark matter finds a way back into the cosmos, causing chaos. Dark matter is what maintains the balance within the Hypersphere. The god manifests himself on earth as a hell-spawned dragon.

The Celestials. The Celestials are powerful sorcerer lords who have obtained god-like status from an otherwise extinct civilisation in the Netherworlds who gained access to the cosmos. In millennia past, the host waged a great war with the Elder God and banished him to the Ghost worlds. Now they execute the will of the Omnisoul, although at times some of them are able to maintain some independence in their actions.

They are seven in number:

The Master – leader of the Celestials, able to commune with the Omnisoul

The Watcher – keeps a careful watch on the Charon, the only beings who pose a threat to their power

The Keeper – The gaoler of the Charon, he keeps them locked in Limbo

The Stalker – The one who finds the Charon to bring back to Limbo after they have served their purpose. Often accompanied by three ravens, symbolic of bad omens and valuable lessons learned

The Sleeper – The only one who returns the Charon to Limbo and who can probably help the Charon find rest

The Guardian – The one who keeps guard over the Well at the Centre of Time, in order to protect the cosmos

The Voice – The only one who communicates with the Charon, in order for them to carry out the will of the Omnisoul

The Charon. The Charon (pronounced Kair-uhn or Karon), meaning fierce brightness, have many guises; they are the Seven Sublime Lords; the first seven manifestations to form within the consciousness of the Omnisoul and are the cosmic agents of change. They are considered by humans to be the great unholy ones, terrifyingly evil and with no mercy or compassion; the first seven breaths of the fiery dragon of wisdom. They are also known to humans as **The Infernal Dukes of Hell** or **The Beautiful and the Damned** – damned because they are immortal and have little life of their own. They are held captive by the Omnisoul, and are used to carry out the will of the Omnisoul as directed by the Celestials.

The Charon:

Adonai the Almighty – Master of the Charon. He is the most ferocious of the Charon with a blood lust that shows no mercy. Death and destruction are left in his wake. His beautiful face with its fine features is in paradox with his hugely muscular and powerful body. In some cultures, Adonai simply means 'my Lord' or 'Master'.

Devi the Scarlet – The female aspect of the divine and counterpart of Adonai, the sacred force or empowerment of the primordial cosmic energy and dynamic forces that move through the entire cosmos. She is terrifyingly fierce and yet sombre. Devi means 'goddess' or 'divine' from the root *'div'* (to shine). In some cultures, Devi is seen as a cosmic force, where she destroys demonic forces that threaten world equilibrium, and creates, annihilates, and recreates the universe.

Aryas the Lord of the Abyss – Aryas is the most noble and exalted of the Charon. He is a flamboyant dandy with an elaborate wardrobe, a sense of humour and sorcerous powers and therefore, a spiritual warrior, skilled in the dark arts and the use of psychedelic herbs. His cosmic oneness is the most developed. Aryas means 'noble'.

Tara the Destroyer – She is the counterpart of Aryas and is known for her wisdom. By meditating and becoming one with the cosmos, she can commune with the music of the spheres. Tara means 'star'; she is the bright fierce annihilator of obstacles whose skill with a sword is unsurpassed by any of the other Charon.

Atman the Grim – He is the most beautiful and melancholy of the Charon. He is the thoughtful quiet one who, despite his nature, has little appetite for death and destruction. He seldom speaks, but when he does, the others listen. In some cultures, he is thought of as the world soul, the inner essence of the universe because Atman is derived from 'ēt-man' meaning 'breath', being one of the first seven breaths of the fiery dragon of wisdom. He is the eternal core of life, helping to release people from their bonds of existence.

Darshan the Invincible – She is a vision of the divine. Appearing serene, she is the most laid back and calm of the Charon until during battle, where blood-lust can sometimes take over. She is the counterpart of Atman. Darshan is derived from the term meaning 'sight' or 'vision' due to her sudden appearances to unsuspecting humans. It is due to this that some cultures regard Darshan as an event of the consciousness.

Paladin the Reaver – He is simply named after his profession.

He is the holy swordsman, skilled in all aspects of war, a massive, formidable sight in his huge and ancient armour, which increases his strength ten-fold, making him the most powerful among the Charon.

Throughout various times and events in history, the Charon have been known individually by other names. The most well-known of these is that of **Lucifer**, the light bringer, the obvious reference being to 'Charon' meaning fierce brightness; this is probably Adonai.

The male members of the Charon are identified with **The Four Horsemen of the Apocalypse**. In the Book of Revelation, the apocalyptic document has seven seals. When the first four are opened, the four horsemen are summoned:

"I watched as the Lamb opened the first of the seven seals. Then I heard one of the four living creatures say in a voice like thunder, 'Come and see.' I looked, and there before me was a white horse. Its rider held a bow, and he was given a crown, and he rode out as a conqueror bent on conquest." This is **Pestilence (Atman)**.

"When the Lamb opened the second seal, I heard the second living creature say, 'Come and see.' Then another horse came out, a fiery red one. Its rider was given power to take peace from the earth and to make men slay each other. To him was given a large sword." This is **War (Adonai)**.

"When the Lamb opened the third seal, I heard the third living creature say, 'Come and see.' I looked, and there before me was a black horse. Its rider was holding a pair of scales in his hand. Then I heard what sounded like a voice among the four living creatures, saying, 'A quart of wheat for a day's wages, and three quarts of barley for a day's wages, and do not damage the oil and the wine'" This is **Famine (Aryas)**.

"When the Lamb opened the fourth seal, I heard the voice of the fourth living creature say, 'Come and see.' I looked and there before me was a pale horse. Its rider was named Death, and Hades was following close behind him. They were given power over a fourth of the earth to kill by sword, famine and plague, and by the wild beasts of the earth." This is **Death**, generally depicted holding a scythe **(Paladin)**.

The female members of the Charon are **Valkyries**. In Norse mythology, a Valkyrie is one of a host of female figures who ride over battlefields selecting the heroic dead to carry off to the afterlife. Some scholars suggest Valkyries were likely originally viewed as demons of the dead to whom warriors slain on the battlefield belonged. Three well known Valkyries listed in the Norse eddas (poems): **Gunnr** (meaning war – **Devi**); **Hildr** (meaning battle – **Tara**) and **Brynhildr** (meaning bright-battle – **Darshan**). It is these three Valkyries who are part of the Charon.

Duranki. Ragnar of Roc was from the land of the Duranki. From the ancient Sumerian term for the people who were created by their Gods. *Dur* translates as *'to Bond'*, *An* translates as *'Heaven'* or *'skies'*, *Ki* translates as *'Earth'*. They were a people bound between heaven and the earth. According to creation myths of the Sumerian people, their Gods used genetic material from life existing on Earth and mixed it with divine genetic material from themselves to create humans here on Earth.

Enoch Slipnot. An anagram of the author's name – Colin Sephton. Enoch is the author of the manuscript Ignatius reads in the Bodleian Library that tells him about the danger that was brought forth by those trained in the art of Al Kimiya in the Land of the Duranki and of the Charon and the cosmic Great Cycle.

The Field. When Ignatius and Indigo are talking to the

elderly Ti-Bottan priest, he tells them that there is no distinction between the material world and the spiritual world. The mechanics of science and spiritualism are one – consciousness and matter are indistinguishable. There is an energy field that entangles and connects everything in the cosmos. Therefore, all life is the resultant coalescence of this energy. Every cubic centimetre of apparently empty space contains an enormous amount of energy. Physicists call it the zero-point energy, because it exists even at absolute zero on the temperature scale. Everything everywhere has a zero-point energy, from particles to electromagnetic fields. The energy of all fields in space is collectively called the zero-point field, known by some as simply the Field.

This field has the potential to provide the universal basis for consciousness from which conscious systems acquire their qualities. On this basis, therefore, awareness is woven into the fabric of the background field, implying that the fundamental mechanism underlying conscious systems rests upon the access to information available in the zero-point field. Evidence suggests the brain produces streams of consciousness by periodically writing information into the zero-point field. It also means that everything in the universe is connected.

Ghost Worlds. The worlds hidden in the additional six dimensions of Calabi-Yau space. They lie outside of the cosmos. Calabi-Ya is banished to them.

The Hypersphere. The Hypershpere is the overall encompassing entirety that is the cosmos. It is the full consciousness of the Omnisoul and contains all that is. The central shell contains our universe and other, unique and sometimes parallel universes, all making what is known as the Multiverse. Linking these universes are the Astral Planes that cross and entangle the planes of existence.

The Shadow Worlds inhabit the Astral Planes.

Towards the outer regions of the cosmic shell are the Netherworlds, the oldest worlds that have drifted outwards due to expansion. Little is known about some of these worlds.

Outside of the cosmic shell is Limbo, the forgotten thoughts of the Omnisoul. This is inhabited by the Ghost Worlds.

Nothing else exists outside of the Hypersphere. However, it is it is possible that there may be a Megasphere containing more than one Hypersphere.

Indigo Gemstone. Indigo is a vision of elegance and grace and a member of the Union Jacks. Beautiful, tall and athletic she is an expert swordswoman. She is feisty and fearless, never afraid of a battle if necessary, serving her nation and the British Empire well. Although she is a popular figure around Oxford, nobody is sure if Indigo Gemstone is her real name. Although she wears a traditional bodice paired with a skirt adorned with numerous embroideries and trims over layers of petticoats, she often wears pinstripe breeches tucked into her boots and a tight-fitting corset. But whatever she is wearing, she is usually expert at concealing a host of steam weapons, derringers or short swords.

Infinity Shards. When Adonai attempts to destroy time, his actions cause time and space to split and produce identical copies of itself. These are called infinity shards. This idea is based on the idea of the Holographic Universe. Some scientists believe the universe is nothing more than an illusion or a giant hologram made up of projections from a level of reality beyond time and space.

When a hologram is cut in two, the whole image can still be seen in each piece. This is because each point in a hologram contains information about light scattered from every point in the image. Therefore, when Adonai tries to destroy the cosmos, it splits into an infinite number of identical pieces. With identical copies of the cosmos comes identical copies of everything within it, including the Charon. Therefore, The Charon are now immortal in infinite worlds, so their attempt to end their own existence has caused even greater complications for their immortality. The hologram idea also helps explain the quantum mechanics theory that information cannot be destroyed and solves the black hole information loss problem, where originally it was thought that anything lost in a black hole is destroyed.

Isambard Ignatius. Isambard Hastings Raffles Ignatius is a tall muscular young man with a shock of blond hair that looks permanently wind swept. Dashingly handsome, he wears an engineer's waistcoat that conceals several steam-powered weapons, including a steam cannon, and he carries a large silver pocket watch and chain. He has a brilliant complex mind and is an engineering genius. He is an explorer and Master of the Chapter of the House of Albion, which is the oldest chapter in the Union. He is also Grand Master of The Union Jacks.

Jeeva. The mighty runesword. The name is from Jiva. In Hinduism and Jainism, a jiva (alternative spelling jeev) is a living being, or any entity imbued with a life force. In Jainism, jiva is the immortal essence or soul of a living organism, which survives physical death. The concept of Ajiva in Jainism means "not soul", and represents matter (including body), time, space, non-motion and motion. Therefore, the unknown god Jeeva who sacrifices himself at the hands of the Norn's smith passes his lifeforce on to become the runesword.

Kaylasa. The central mountain peak of the crater that hides the city of Sagharta. From Mount Kailasa (or Kailash), which is believed by Hindus to be the home of Siva. Kailasa is said to be at the centre of six mountain ranges, forming a lotus, and it is also said to be the source of four sacred rivers flowing into India.

Magus. A member of a priestly caste of ancient Persia. An astrologer, sorcerer, or magician. The leader of the demon hunters. The name is used in irony, given it means sorcerer and he is hunting demons, accusing the prostitute of being one.

Mahkali. Leader of the Skin Scribes. The name derives from Mahakhali, the literal meaning of which translates as Great Kali, the Hindu Goddess, considered by some to be the consort of Shiva, and by others as the basis of Reality. Kali is a destroyer.

Maya. Maya has multiple meanings in Indian philosophies, depending on the context. In ancient Vedic literature, Maya implies extraordinary power and wisdom. In later Vedic texts and modern literature dedicated to Indian traditions, Maya denotes an illusion where things appear to be present but are not what they seem. It is perceived reality, one that does not reveal the hidden principles, the true reality. When the Charon find Skye, they think she is able to open the Book of Consciousness because she is either born of Calabi-Ya or she is able to separate herself from the Maya, from the illusion of life.

Norns. In Norse mythology, the Norns are female beings who rule the destiny of gods and men. They are similar to the Fates of Greek mythology. They are three sisters – Skel, Verani, and Uror – the personifications of the past, present and future. The names used are derived from the Norse Skuld (being), Verdandi (necessity), and Urd (fate).

The Omnisoul. In the beginning there was Existence alone – One only, without a second. The One thought "Let me be many, let me grow forth." Thus, out of The Omnisoul projected the cosmos, and having projected out, entered into every being. All that is has its self in the Omnisoul. The Omnisoul created the Hypershere. The movement of the stars and planets is governed by the laws of vibration and rhythm that are played out by the energy field of the Omnisoul and the Cosmic Sitar. According to the laws of physics, all cosmic matter can manifest as particles and waves. These waves are the resultant vibration of the mental thoughts of the Omnisoul and form the harmonic geometry of the cosmos. The interference of these mental waves is viewed as particles, which means that all matter can be shaped by sound and thought vibration. The Hypershere is the entanglement of the Omnisoul's consciousness. Whenever the harmony of the cosmos is lacking in any way, the Omnisoul plays music and order can be restored. The Omnisoul *is* the Hypershere. The Omnisoul is indescribable, eternal, omnipotent, omniscient and omnipresent, the only Truth and the First Cause. The Omnisoul is not a God, but rather the ultimate, unexplainable principle encompassing all of creation.

Omphalos. The Temple of the Dawn is called Omphalos, meaning 'navel'. It is the centre of the cosmos. The Temple houses the Well at the Centre of Time (Yukteswar).

Qanun. A qanun (kanun, ganoun or kanoon) is a stringed musical instrument originating in Assyria. A qanun is played by plucking strings and is usually played on the lap while sitting or squatting.

Ragnar of Roc. The wizard Ragnar of Roc is a play on Ragnarok from Norse mythology. Its meaning is 'The Doom of the Gods' and is the end of the mythical cycle, during which the cosmos is destroyed and is subsequently re-created. The arrival of Calabi-Ya from the Ghost Worlds has the potential to destroy parts of the cosmos.

Sagharta. Sagharta is a cathedral-like edifice soaring high into the sky. The city is built with monolithic wind harps on its upper arches, which moan loudly in the chill wind, striking fear into anyone who should ever find the city. Surrounding the city is the Lake of the Celestial Lotus, into which runs the River of Woe. It is said the River of Woe links the earth with the underworld, where the Charon dwell.

The name derives from Agartha (sometimes Agartta, Agharti, Agarta or Agarttha), a legendary city said to be located in the Earth's core. It is related to the belief in a hollow Earth and is sometimes believed to be a vast complex of caves underneath Tibet. Agartha is frequently associated or confused with Shambhala, a mythical kingdom hidden somewhere in Asia (sometimes Shambala or Shamballa). It gradually became to be seen as a pure and fabulous land whose reality is visionary or spiritual as much as physical or geographic. Other scriptures speak of a closely related land called Tagzig Olmo Lung Ring, a spiritual realm, plane or dimension.

Samardi. Samardi is the name of the Cosmic Sitar. The name is from the Hindu Samadhi which means 'to bring together' or the perfect union of the individualised soul with the infinite spirit. The runesword Jeeva was brought together with the Guardian's sitar to create the Cosmic Sitar Samardi. Samadhi is a state of intense concentration achieved through meditation. In yoga, this is regarded as the final stage, at which union with the divine is reached (before or at death). It was used as the name of the sitar as it is about to be used to bring about the end of the Charon.

Satvaguna. The place where the sword Jeeva resides with the Norns. Its name derives from Sattva which is one of the three Gunas (tendencies, qualities, attributes). Sattva is the Guna which makes us happy and gives us clear knowledge. Sattva Guna is a force favourable for the attainment of Moksha, which in Hindu philosophy refers to various forms of emancipation, liberation, and release from bondage.

Shanka. The Omnisoul sounded the great conch shell Shanka to mark the passing of the current time. The name is from the Hindu Shankha, which symbolises the origin of the universe from a single source. Being found in water, it represents the causal water from which the universe was evolved and into which it gets dissolved. When blown, it produces a sound that represents the primeval sound, from which creation developed.

Skye.   Skye can open the great Book of Consciousness. She infiltrated the Union Jacks in order to acquire the book for the Elder God. She is the leader of a little-known underground cult thriving in Oxford. She carries the oppressive burden of a dark secret that has been the long heritage of her family. She is of the Angevin blood line or the House of Anjou, her particular line dating back to Richard I, the Lionhearted. Legend has it that the House of Anjou were descended from no less a person than Satan.

King Richard, cursed as infernal by Saladin, produced no legitimate heirs, and despite history recording Richard as a homosexual, he acknowledged an illegitimate son, Philip of Cognac. But Richard also had an illegitimate daughter who, like the Pharaohs of ancient Egypt where descent was through the female line, continued the Angevin bloodline through to the present day. Legend has it that the Templars conversed with an idol called Baphomet. Richard coupled with the female consort of Baphomet and illegitimate hell-spawn was produced, surviving to this day. These hell-spawn are destined to live a miserable existence, doom-trodden and self-destructive. An infestation upon the earth that one day, given the right circumstances, they have the potential to rise and conquer nations. Or just simply bring large-scale death and bloody destruction to the earth. But as yet, the circumstances had never been quite right for a full demonic deluge, and so the blood line continues to wait and watch, ready to seize the right moment.

Due to the circumstances of her upbringing, Skye had tried to find solace in all sorts of depravity to fulfil her dark cravings. It was like a giant self-destruct button had been pressed. Not content with hallucinogens and swigging absinthe neat from the bottle, she had begun to experiment with occult rituals and the casting of runes to determine her next actions. Runes, she said, spoke of the beginning of all time. By means of her runic knowledge, Skye could find hidden meanings in all things and in particular, meanings in sounds. Upon her left breast, she had tattooed the master of all runes, the Black Sun. Her Black Order had adopted it as their emblem. Skye was not on any mission for The Union – that was just her cover; she was looking to the fate of her own blood line.

Taraka. Taraka is the name of the Charon's ship. Taraka is derived from the Sanskrit tāraka meaning crossing or ferryman. It was used as the name for the Charon's ship as they are the ferryman from Greek mythology. In Hindu the name can also mean star, so it is also appropriate as the ship travels the cosmos.

The Ti-botta. The Ti-botta live upon the earth in the land of fire and ice. It is a strange mystical land that exists across more than one plane and therefore cannot be found easily, sometimes fading in and out of the planes it crosses. Sometimes it exists on the present-day earth (whenever that is) and at times on an alternative earth. Due to the ghostly property of the kingdom, and the fragility of the planes it crosses, the land is fissured with deep crevasses where molten lava flows forth from the earth, giving the name the Land of Fire and Ice.

The land is surrounded and protected by a ring of snow-capped mountain peaks that are the remnants of a meteorite crater. The great mystical city of Sagharta is built upon the central peak.

The Ti-Botta are ancient priest-like warriors, the heralds of the Charon upon the earth, practitioners of esoteric practices and masters of consciousness, which explains the most repeated symbol in their land – the all-seeing eyes of the Ti-Botta. They are capable of summoning the Charon, but seldom do so as a summoning usually ends in death; The Charon show no mercy, even to those who revere them.

Dotted around are smaller temples and platforms for meditation. These are usually found in the icy wind-swept wilderness and are marked by prayer flags, the only movement that disturbs the tranquillity. The Ti-Botta are based on the Tibetans.

Turiya. Turiya is the name of the Book of Consciousness. In Hindu philosophy, turiya is pure consciousness. Turiya is the background that underlies and transcends the three common states of consciousness. These are waking, dreaming, and dreamless sleep.

The Union Jacks. The Union Jacks are a secret organisation, invisible and omnipresent, without beginning or end; with no recognised recorded history. They are individuals of Engineering Science, technological masters without borders. Their story is long and complex, and entwined with the established history. The secret Brotherhood that preceded them traced their origins to Brutus of Troy.

The modern-day Union traces its origins back to circa 1275, obtaining a Royal Charter in 1775, their remit being to defend the interests of the Empire in British America, eventually expanding to defending all the interests of the British Empire.

Their number, rank and file is unknown and unknowable. However, three are known to be operating in Oxford. Their Grand Master is Isambard Ignatius, a brilliant scientist and engineer from Oxford University.

Yukteswar. Yukteswar is the Well at the Centre of Time. Yukteswar is a Sanskrit term, which refers to becoming united with God. The Well at the Centre of Time is the navel of the cosmos and is linked directly to the Omnisoul, therefore, by trying to destroy it The Charon are trying to destroy the power of the Omnisoul. The well is the first spark of consciousness that was cast into the heavens by the Omnisoul to form this Hypersphere. It once lay at the centre of the Hypershpere and is still represented as such on maps of the cosmos, however, due to cosmic expansion, its location has been lost and it drifts randomly through the cosmos entangling the threads of the thirty-one planes of existence. It is sometimes called the Golden Womb, the Cosmic Egg or the Navel of the Hypersphere, it is the place of its creation. The well is on a planet that does not rotate, it is the stillest place in the Hypersphere. It is housed in a great temple, the entrance to which is marked by two great pillars. It lies on the shores of the unknown and is known as Omphalos the Temple of the Dawn. The well is represented as an enormous singing bowl that resonates out across the entire Hypersphere when struck.

The Union Jacks – Some Historical Background

The time of Ignatius and Indigo is set in the steam-driven world of the British Empire. This tiny seafaring nation with the spirit of John Bull that gave the world the greatest and largest empire in history covering about a quarter of the world's population is run and governed by what has become known as the Island Race.

Britain, founded by Brutus after the battle of Troy and once the home of Albion the giant, was the land where Saint George slew the dragon and was peopled by the Lost Tribes of Dan, Benjamin and Judah. It is said to be protected by Britannia and the Lion of Judah, giving its monarchy divine right. It was once home to the Pendragons, the greatest of whom was King Arthur, and it has continued ever since with a long secret history of protectors that watch over the Empire still today. They are known simply as the Union Jacks.

Founded to protect and to serve this Sceptered Isle, whomever they are, they are invisible and omnipresent, without beginning or end, individuals of Engineering and Science, technological masters without borders. Their story is long and complex, entwined with the established history, tracing their original brotherhood directly back to Brutus and beyond. But you will not find any such history in the known books.

The Age of Albion

The chapter house for which Ignatius is Grand Master is called Albion, after the original name for Britain. Some believe the name Albion (or insula Albionum), comes from either the Latin albus meaning white (referring to the first view of Britain from the continent, the white cliffs of Dover) or the "island of the Albiones", first mentioned in the Massaliote Periplus, a merchants' handbook now lost to history.

Albion was a giant, and the fourth son of Neptune and Amphitrite, who both loved him more than any of their other children. He came from the wild frozen wastes of Hyperborea far to the north wherein dwelled winged Boreas, the god of the cold north wind and the bringer of winter. It was a land inhabited by giants who were quite used to the harsh wintery climate.

When it came time for him to receive a kingdom, Neptune consulted all the mermaids and mermen to look for an island for him to rule over. All tried and failed, until the last mermaid, who was more beautiful than any other, came to consult Neptune and his council. She took them to a small green island with its mountains and valleys, white cliffs and golden sands. As soon as Neptune saw it, he announced that this was the island for his beloved son, and it would be named after him.

There he ruled over the island, until eventually he ventured into Gaul (France) to oppose the progress of Hercules in his western march and was slain by him during a great battle.

The Age of Brutus

In truth, nobody knows the true ancient history of Great Britain. After the story of Albion, legend has it that the fearless inhabitants of this noble island descended from Brutus.

Epic poems tell that in the great sea to the south, shadows moved across the earth and nations fought each other. Whole civilisations and great cities fell due to human greed and jealousies. One such war broke out between the Achaeans and the Trojans, (1194–1184 BCE, according to Eratosthenes, or c. 1250 BCE according to Herodotus). Paris of Troy stole Helen from the King of Sparta, Menelaus. Calling upon his alliances, Menelaus asked Agamemnon, king of Mycenae, to assist in retrieving Helen, and a great war raged. Eventually the city of Troy fell, the Achaens laying waste to their lands. The few survivors escaped under the leadership of a warrior called Brute (Brutus), the son of Silvius and great grandson of Aeneas. Brutus was instructed by a vision of the goddess Diana to lead a band of exiles from Troy to the land of Albion.

After setting sail for north Africa and then Gaul, they eventually travelled further west beyond the Pillars of Hercules, landing eventually in Albion, in the town of Totnes. The island was desert and inhospitable, occupied only by a remnant of the giant race whose excessive force and tyranny had destroyed much of the land. The Trojans encountered these and eradicated them. Brutus, keen to establish a city for themselves, founded Troia Nova (New Troy) on the banks of the river Thames, corrupted by later legions to Trinovantum, eventually becoming what is now London.

The lords made Brutus their master, and so Albion became Britain (or Brittia), named after him, and Brutus ruled for twenty-four years, giving a part of the land in the southwest to his greatest warrior, Corineus and that part became known as Corinee (Cornwall). This created the first Union of Albion.

The story of Brutus and the Trojans is reinforced when one examines the history of the Celts, who were wide-spread throughout Europe. The Celts and their variously named tribes and sub-races are first found in the very area into which the captive Ten Tribes of the Northern House of Israel disappeared. Some members of the Ten Tribes left exile and moved westwards and northwards into what we know as Armenia, then to a place called Ar-Sareth.

The later immigrants, the Franks, from whom France takes its name, are said to originate in Phrygia, which was territory near Troy in present-day Turkey. It would appear that they also are descendants of the Trojans in France, for the tribe that founded Paris were the Parisi (the Trojan War was caused by the abduction of Helen by Paris). There is also Troyes, which must have been named for the old homeland of the Parisi.

The Tribe of Benyamin (or Benjamin) was the smallest tribe in Judea and the most warlike. Most of Benyamin's people remained in Asia (Russia) then migrated over the Caucus mountains into

Europe. They joined the two brother Tribes of Ephraim and Manasseh in Europe. Brutus descended from the tribe of Benyamin.

A region of Turkey used to be called "Dardania," and one of the narrow straits between the Aegean Sea and the Black Sea by Russia is still called Dardanelles. They are named after the tribe of Dan. At about the time of the Assyrian captivity (c. 720 BCE), the sea-faring Danites sailed with the Simeonites to the British Isles and settled in Ireland and the Tribe of Simeon settled on the west coast of Scotland gradually migrating southward and settling in Wales. The other tribes arrived in 449 CE.

Other etymology, still linked to the lost tribes, suggests that the island's name comes from the word Berith, which is the Hebrew word for covenant, and Ish is the Hebrew word for man. By combining the two words, the word Berith-ish (Covenant Man) is formed, providing the basis for the word British.

Yet another alternative history is that Histion, the son of Japhet and grandson of Noah, had four sons – Francus, Romanus, Alemannus, and Britto – from whom descended the French, Roman, German, and British peoples.

Whatever, the truth, the long and rich ancestry continues with the Union Jacks, who are sworn to protect the land where the sun never sets, led by its greatest warriors, Ignatius and Indigo.